The frog h[...]e, and now be[...]

She slid him anoth[...] Oscar had filled ou[...] youthful skinniness giving way to a broadness of shoulder and a depth of chest that had never occurred to Molly he would achieve. He'd always been tall, but with the long sticklike legs of a crane.

Now she could see the large muscles of his thigh being molded by the fabric of dark denim. His jacket, draped around her shoulders, was expensive, and in taking it off he'd revealed a crisp white dress shirt, open at the throat. He had on a leather belt that matched the buff of his brown leather shoes.

The sophisticated haircut showed off the lines of his face: the wide, intelligent forehead, the straight nose, extraordinary cheekbones, full, sensual lips.

Lips I'd tasted. Kissed. In that one moment that had changed everything. Had she come here thinking she could put that behind her? That they could just be the best of friends again?

His Cinderella
Next Door

—

Cara Colter

Recycling programs
for this product may
not exist in your area.

ISBN-13: 978-1-335-56703-1

His Cinderella Next Door

Copyright © 2021 by Cara Colter

This edition published by arrangement with Harlequin Books S.A.

For questions and comments about the quality of this book,
please contact us at CustomerService@Harlequin.com.

Harlequin Enterprises ULC
22 Adelaide St. West, 40th Floor
Toronto, Ontario M5H 4E3, Canada
www.Harlequin.com

Printed in U.S.A.

Cara Colter shares her life in beautiful British Columbia, Canada, with her husband, nine horses and one small Pomeranian with a large attitude. She loves to hear from readers, and you can learn more about her and contact her through Facebook.

Books by Cara Colter

Harlequin Romance

A Fairytale Summer!

Cinderella's New York Fling

Cinderellas in the Palace

His Convenient Royal Bride
One Night with Her Brooding Bodyguard

A Crown by Christmas

Cinderella's Prince Under the Mistletoe

The Vineyards of Calanetti

Soldier, Hero...Husband?

Snowbound with the Single Dad
Tempted by the Single Dad
Matchmaker and the Manhattan Millionaire

Visit the Author Profile page
at Harlequin.com for more titles.

Praise for
Cara Colter

"Ms. Colter's writing style is one you will want to continue to read. Her descriptions place you there.... This story does have a HEA but leaves you wanting more."

—*Harlequin Junkie* on *His Convenient Royal Bride*

CHAPTER ONE

Come.

MOLLY BENTWELL CLOSED her eyes. How could a single word evoke so much feeling? The word removed her—thankfully and completely—from the chaos all around her.

Her small Frankfurt flat currently looked as though it had been burglarized. Boxes were stacked haphazardly. Clothes were strewn on the floor. There were bright empty squares on the walls, where the paint had not faded, where not so long ago all the pictures had hung.

She was getting ready to move, again. She wasn't quite sure where. Paris was too expensive. Ditto for London.

It didn't really matter where, though. Moving was an excellent antidote for pain.

She closed her eyes against the fresh wave of hurt that hit her. Ralphie was gone. Even now, eight months, one week and two days later, it seemed impossible.

He had been the one constant in her life. He had been the one it was safe to love. Every single day, no matter where her photography had taken her, he had been her touchstone. She would check the time differences and it didn't matter if it was the middle of the night where she was, if it was eight in the morning where he was, she called.

And the sun came out in her world when she heard his voice. When he told her news of Georgie, the cat he'd inherited from her.

The first thing Molly had done, in every single destination she had arrived at, was take a photograph of some special thing like an alligator, an elephant, a flower or a tree. Mostly she emailed them, and Ralphie would reply to the email with a picture of the cat that was beloved to both of them.

Now, the message she had grown up with—that love was the most dangerous thing of all—had been reinforced in the most terrible way.

She opened her eyes, and that single word jumped out of the email in front of her again.

Come.

The word filled her with longing to be with him. Oscar Clark, Ralphie's brother, the only other person in the world who would totally get the sharp ache of this never-ending pain.

Oscar. Truck, she'd called him the first day they'd met, in kindergarten. She'd been reading since she was four, and she had picked the word *car* out of his carefully printed name on his bright yellow sunshine-shaped tag.

"Truck is a better name," she'd informed him, full of the officiousness of being the only one in the kindergarten class who already knew how to read. "My daddy says he would never own a car. Never."

And so, Truck it was.

As it turned out, Oscar lived on the estate next to the ramshackle farm that Molly and her father, Jimmy, used as a home base when Jimmy wasn't working on a film as one of the most sought-after stuntmen in the industry. Her mother, who had died when Molly was very young, was a vague memory of good smells and soft words read from a large picture book. Her mother was also Jimmy's cautionary tale to his daughter about the dangers of love.

"Beware of love," he'd tell her, made melancholy by a few drinks. "It is hiding daggers in its magical cloak."

And he'd been right. Because she had loved him, her father—and all of his magic and chaos—madly, and still felt the dagger of that loss in her heart daily.

Now, Ralphie.

And now, Oscar, asking her to come. She was aware of wanting what he promised—comfort, commiseration—with a yearning that was both compelling and frightening.

She thought, again, of that first day of school. Standing there, in the classroom, Molly had already been aware she was different than the other children, and not because she was the only one who knew how to read. The girls were in pretty dresses and had ribbons in their curled locks. All the children had a shiny fresh-scrubbed look about them. Nobody else's father was there.

Molly was in bib overalls, with a rip in one knee and a brand new white T-shirt, with which she had been inordinately pleased. Her dad had clumsily contained her unruly mop of curly hair into a braid so tight it felt as if her skin were being stretched. She had bathed last night, but on the way to school, her hand firmly in her father's—terrified of this strange institution she was being turned over to—she had seen a frog. And had to have it.

Her dad had helped her catch it and put it in his pocket for her to have later because, according to him, frogs weren't allowed in school.

This astonishing declaration intensified Molly's feeling of being sent to some kind of joyless dungeon, like the ones princesses in fairy tales so often ended up in.

Molly and her father presented themselves to the kindergarten teacher thirty minutes late, and with smudges of mud puddle on their faces and hands. Her new T-shirt was nowhere near white anymore.

Halfway through that torturous first morning, the frog had decided to announce his escape from her father's pocket with giant hops down the row between the desks, croaking loudly, and relieving the pure tedium of learning the words for colors, which Molly already knew.

Miss Michaels jumped on her chair in an astounding show of hysteria. The girls in the class, apparently looking to Miss Michaels for what Molly already considered somewhat dubious leadership, began to scream.

The boys abandoned their seats and took after the frog, creating pandemonium. Soon, the classroom floor was littered with papers and books, pencils and crayons, one overturned desk and a broken chair.

He'd emerged with the frog—that boy with the big glasses and the sun-shaped name tag that said *Oscar* on it—and held it to his chest, protectively, away from the other boys. Truck had held that frog with tenderness that won Molly's young heart.

If she were a princess confined to a dungeon, he was the prince who would rescue her.

They had been friends ever since. Oscar was quiet, smart, steady, the class geek, even in kindergarten, and Molly was the bold one, the rambunctious one, the one who was always either in trouble or looking for it.

And then there had been his brother, Ralphie, the third member of their circle. Her throat closed as she remembered his laughter, and she felt a sting behind her eyes. Eight months, one week and two days. How was Oscar surviving the loss?

Come.

Even now, a world away, six years from the last time she had seen him, Molly could feel the longing for the comfort of his presence, the steadiness of him, the feeling of being safe and cared about, liked exactly as she was.

Those feelings crowded out a sense of danger that had entered their relationship unexpectedly. When her prince had kissed her, making them both aware of each other in a new way.

A way that had made her understand love

had a dimension to it that was as terrifying as her father had so dourly warned her all those years.

Looking at Oscar's invitation now, Molly was aware all those feelings he evoked in her—not to mention the added dimension—should be the exact thing she should run away from right now.

But life had stolen her strength. Molly let her eyes drop to the temptation of the next line.

I've broken up with Cynthia. Why don't you come to Vancouver for a few days? My place is huge. We could just hang out and have some fun, and do what best friends do, which is help each other through a rough time. I don't know how I'm going to handle Ralphie's birthday.

Just like that, she could picture Oscar, the way he had been when she last saw him, tall and lanky, like a puppy who had not yet grown into its feet. That shock of dark hair—*the perfect mad scientist doo*, she used to call it affectionately—falling down over one eye. Oblivious to peer pressure—you could afford that when you were born a Clark—he was always dressed as if his clothes were an absent-minded afterthought. She had seen him have on shorts in the winter, or different colored socks. Occasionally, his shoes didn't match, either. Sometimes his shirts were inside out.

When one of those popular girls—why did they always have such mean eyes—had tried to mock him for that inside-out shirt, he had looked down at himself with surprised interest and said, ever so mildly, "In Belize, they would say I am hunting witches."

Who knew that kind of thing? Oscar, that's who.

Six years since she had seen him. She felt the ache of missing him. But after her father's death, life had changed so quickly, her world had been upended so fast. She'd learned the hard way about love's daggers. And her feelings for Oscar... Molly frowned. She didn't want to think of that anymore.

As much as she had embraced keeping in touch with Ralphie, she had kept things deliberately at a distance with Oscar.

They sent each other the odd email, he always called her on her birthday, and she always called him on his, they exchanged Christmas gifts each year, the funnier the better. She usually added to his beloved, and ever so nerdy, science T-shirt collection, and he usually found her the worst photographs imaginable and had them elaborately framed.

Those photographs always hung in places

of honor wherever she lived. Now, she'd taken them off the walls in preparation for her latest move.

She looked back to Oscar's email.

I need to do something for Ralphie. His birthday would be a good time, but I don't know what to do. I'm lost.

She had always counted on Oscar to be unchanging; she had relied on his steadiness. He was lost? It seemed unimaginable.

But she felt lost, too, ever since he had called her to tell her Ralphie had died. She had planned to go home for the service, but it turned out Mrs. Clark, Ralphie and Oscar's mother, had decided against a service. But how did they arrive at closure without that important marking place? Without holding some occasion to celebrate Ralphie's too-short life?

Molly let her eyes drop to the final line of the email.

I need you.

She had always needed Oscar—even from afar, his steadiness was there, in the background—but had he ever needed her before?

Come.

It felt as if she were a sailor on a boat that had been tossed about by a stormy sea and suddenly, by way of Oscar's unexpected invitation, she had spotted a lighthouse.

She clicked on the attachment that Oscar had sent with the email.

Molly wasn't sure what she was expecting. A recent picture of him, perhaps?

Her jaw fell. It was a first-class ticket to Vancouver from Frankfurt. It had her name on it and tomorrow's date.

She stared at it.

She couldn't possibly go. But why not? The move could wait. She hadn't given notice, yet. She was undecided exactly where to go, anyway.

Maybe being around Oscar's steadiness would help her crystalize her own plans for the future.

Ever since she was a child, she had traveled on short notice, and as a photographer, the pattern continued. In fact, she was scheduled to go to Africa at the beginning of next week, so it was not as if her passport was not up to date. She was an absolute expert at throwing a few essentials into the carry-on bag that she prided herself on being able to live out of—anywhere—for a week, or even two.

She glanced around at the mess of unre-
solved issues in her apartment.

She thought of Oscar—Truck. The warmth
in his eyes, the easiness of his smile, his calm
way of being in the world.

She thought of them needing each other to
say a proper goodbye to Ralphie.

She sent a text to her contact in Africa. Molly
hesitated, took a deep breath, hesitated for a
few more seconds, then pushed print on the
airline ticket on her screen. Only after she'd
printed it, did she notice there was no return
flight information.

Molly was a woman who did scary things for
a living. She was a woman who welcomed the
charge of the elephant, and who would eagerly
hang from her knees from the tallest branch of
a tree if it meant getting the picture perfect.

So why did the airline ticket, with no return,
being spit out by her printer, feel like one of the
scariest adventures she would ever embark on?

CHAPTER TWO

"Truck!"

Hearing the name only Molly had ever called him coming through the throngs at Vancouver International Airport, did a funny thing in the region of Oscar's heart. Since his brother had died, it felt as if his heart were a stone in the center of his chest. He didn't want it fluttering back to life.

It was so much easier to feel nothing at all. But if he had wanted to feel nothing at all, why ask Molly, the person who made him feel everything so intensely, to come?

Because she had navigated the sea of grief over her father. Because she had loved Ralphie as dearly as he. There was a hope she would know what to do.

And under that, it was a bit of a test for him. He was a scientist. He enjoyed tests. He needed to prove theories. And his theory—since the death of his brother and the end of his engagement—

was that relationships sucked, and that he would
not be having another one.

No, he would remain single. He would hike
high mountains and explore the world on his
own. No one could show you how to turn life
into an adventure more quickly than Molly
could.

That, and he was pretty sure she was the only
person in the world who understood what he
was feeling for Ralphie.

And it was that mutual love of Ralphie that
made it so he could not hold himself back. He
didn't walk to her. He ran. He scooped her up,
and her weight felt familiar to him, feather-
light, and yet there was that supple strength
as she wrapped her arms around his neck. Her
fragrance denied nine hours or more of travel,
and was intensely familiar, sharp and sweet
at the same time, like high-mountain huckleberries. It made him want to bury his nose
in her hair.

Instead, he swung her around until her
laughter—and his—rang out, joyous.

Finally, he set her down, inspected her
closely. The laughter still lightened her features. Her hair had always been the most remarkable color—like maple syrup in a glass jar,
with the sun shining through it. Her hair was
shorter than he ever remembered it being, but

if cutting it had been an attempt to tame those crazy curls, it had failed. Half of them corkscrewed wildly around her face, and the other half were smooshed to one side.

The darkness of her freckles over her snub of a nose, the faint golden tone of her skin, spoke of a life outdoors, and her eyes were still as green as the lushness of a mountain meadow in spring.

And her lips—those cute little bow lips— were as plump and inviting as a field-grown strawberry. Still, he wasn't going to look at them for too long. Even though it had been six years, he remembered the taste of them, the surge of energy that had gone through him that nothing and no one else in his life had ever replicated.

So, really, he had a mission here that would not be advanced by the study of her lips.

Molly and he were going to say goodbye to his brother together.

Just seeing her again, he was acutely and deliciously aware of how much this friendship meant to him.

"How can you look just the same?" he asked her. "You were eighteen years old the last time I saw you!"

"It was probably the same outfit," she said wryly.

He regarded her: the khakis, the wrinkle-free green shirt that made her eyes look greener, though he was sure that was unintentional.

"I'm pretty sure it *is* the same outfit," he said thoughtfully, and was rewarded with her laugh.

He didn't add that she looked as good— better—in that casual outfit than most women would look in an evening gown.

"You know how I like to shop. Once I find something that works, I just get ten of it. Though sometimes..."

Her voice drifted away, and she looked faintly embarrassed.

"Sometimes, what?"

"I'm just tired."

"No, what?"

She seemed to consider. "I guess sometimes I wonder what it would be like to be a real girl. You know, with a wardrobe that had a dress in it. Like I say, I'm just tired."

He couldn't miss the tiny bit of wistfulness in her voice. It was true that being raised by a single dad she had probably missed many of the feminine touches in her upbringing that her mother would have provided. She had always seemed so secure in herself, that it had never occurred to him before that she might have secretly longed for what other girls took for granted.

He made a note to himself and filed it away.

Molly cocked her head at him and studied him solemnly. "You've changed. A lot."

He lifted an eyebrow. "In what way?"

"You're sophisticated. I think your haircut might be better than mine. No worn high-top running shoes that don't match. I guess I was hoping for a T-shirt that would make me laugh."

"I've got a great new one. It says, Scientists Do it with Energy."

Her blush actually deepened, and he felt a sudden need to change the subject. What had made him say that? The last thing he needed to be thinking about when he was with Molly was *that*. Particularly since he was taking her home.

He wondered, a little too late, if he had thought this thing through enough. The truth was, he hadn't thought it through at all. Molly had always brought out an impulsiveness in Oscar that he usually did not indulge. She had also always been a disruptive force in his ordered life.

"Let's head to the baggage claim."

"I've got it all here. My legacy from Dad, pack quick and tight."

He looked at the medium-sized bag hanging from her shoulder. Even as it underscored his sense that she had not changed—how many women could pack everything they needed for a trip in an overnight bag—he thought he heard a touch of wistfulness again.

From the size of the bag, it looked like her visit wasn't going to be extended. He'd left the ticket open, so she could book her return at her convenience. She was, just as her father had been, a rolling stone. No surprise there.

"I have enough to last me for a while. I didn't actually book a return flight yet. I thought we'd just see how it goes," she said, as though reading his mind.

The part of Oscar that liked order—that needed to know exactly how many groceries to buy, and made reservations weeks or months in advance—cringed at that. But another part of him didn't. Because even though she seemed unchanged, she was right.

He was changed.

He knew, as he had not known before, that efforts to control things, to put them in order, were largely an illusion. The world did what it wanted.

And he was aware he had changed in another way, and that way seemed to involve an acute awareness of her.

"It's probably half cameras," Oscar said, focusing on her bag instead of her.

"I have my travel wardrobe down to an art," she said. She cocked his head at him, and that familiar smile teased her lips. "Or would that be science?"

"Let me take it, at least."

For a moment, she looked as if she might argue, fiercely independent even about such a small thing as surrendering her bag. But then she shrugged it off and gave it to him. There was an odd look on her face. What was it? Could she possibly enjoy being looked after somewhat guiltily?

"I'm looking forward to hearing about some of your travels," Oscar said. And he meant it. Molly Bentwell had always had a way of finding an adventure.

But a little voice in his head insisted on reminding him that she had gone on to have her adventures *without him*.

She had left what they had shared together with the most perfunctory of goodbyes.

This is what he needed in his newly single life: deep friendships, uncomplicated by other agendas. That feeling of being supported and seen, without the complication of other, well, feelings.

Feelings. Pesky things to his scientific mind. Complicated and rife with consequences that couldn't be predicted.

It was raining hard when he held open the door for her. Without thinking about it, he shrugged off his jacket and put it around her shoulders.

For just a moment, that look of familiar stubbornness crossed her face, but then she relaxed and snuggled into the coat.

"Ah, Galahad," she said. "My prince."

"Galahad wasn't a prince," he said. "He was a knight."

"Trust you to know that," she teased him.

If ever there were a woman who made him want to play the part of a knight in shining armor, or a prince riding in to the rescue, it was Molly.

Thankfully, Oscar thought, his pragmatic nature, and the loss of his brother, made him immune to the charms of fairy tales. Plus, she was the woman least likely to ever play the role of anyone's princess.

Outside the airport, Molly paused at Oscar's vehicle. "But it's not a truck," she said.

Oscar shook his head. This was one of the things he remembered best about Molly Bentwell.

He came from a world where every status of wealth and success and accomplishment was collected and displayed, as if that said who you were in the world.

But Molly had always dug deeper, required more.

"The only girl in the world who would look

at a sports car of this caliber and say *that*," he replied dryly.

"It's not that it isn't gorgeous, it's just not what I expected," she said.

He stowed their things and held the door for her, then he got in the car. He couldn't help but show off just a little bit. The car was exquisite in its power and ability to maneuver in and out of choked traffic. The windshield wipers slapped at the rain, and inside it felt cozy and oddly intimate as her scent took over the small area.

"Humph," she said, unimpressed, and apparently not feeling the intimacy at all, thank goodness. "If you can drive a car like this, you could easily drive a truck in this traffic."

"Molly, I don't have any use for a truck."

"Humph."

"What do you drive?"

"I don't have a car. But if I did—"

"It would be a truck," he said, wryly. "You haven't changed your opinion on that since kindergarten."

And then they were both laughing, a familiar ease flowing into place between them. He felt as if he had last spent time with her yesterday, not six years ago. And yet, it had been six years and now there were so many blanks that needed to be filled in.

"How did you end up in Frankfurt, this time?"

"I know it seems weird, what with there not being a wild animal in sight, but it's central, it has a great airport and flights are cheap. Africa would be a couple of days travel from Canada and Asia even longer. So I can get to most of the wild places that are left in the world in pretty short order from where I live. And the biggest market for my photos is European, so it just makes sense."

All the places had made sense, Oscar thought, and yet she never stayed in any of them. She had moved at least six times in the six years since she had been away and he knew it was only a matter of time before she moved again.

She confirmed this by saying, "I'm thinking of moving."

"Again?"

She lifted a slender shoulder and yawned. "I'm feeling restless."

He was pretty sure what she was feeling was pain, pure and simple, just like he was. Could he say to her, *Oh, Molly, there are some things you can't run away from*?

It seemed too personal, the six years of separation yawning between them.

"What time is it, here?"

"Nine p.m. Are you going to have jet lag?"

"No, the secret is to get into your new time

zone as quickly as possible. So, it's five a.m. in Frankfurt. I'm just getting up! I'll be good for a few hours. Did you have a plan for tonight?"

"I do," he said. "It's a surprise."

CHAPTER THREE

MOLLY SLID OSCAR a glance. As if the way he looked wasn't surprising enough!

"I have a surprise for you, too," she said. "But it's a secret. Don't even try to pry it out of me."

"One cinnamon bun, and you'd talk."

"No fair using the secret weapon." The truth was she wanted to tell him, to share her excitement. But no, for once in her life she would keep a secret from him. So far, she had two confirmations and a tentative venue to celebrate the beautiful life that had been Ralphie's. But things could still fall apart, so she would say nothing about it and totally surprise Oscar with it, if it all came together.

She considered the fact that Oscar has planned a surprise for her tonight. Everything about him seemed to be a surprise: the new suave look, the sleek car, her awareness of him. His jacket, settled around Molly's shoulders, was deeply comforting in a way that had little to do with its protection from the damp.

The frog had remained a prince, but now he looked like one, too. She slid him another look, taking in the changes. He had filled out substantially, his youthful skinniness giving way to a broadness of shoulder and a depth of chest it had never occurred to Molly that he would achieve. He'd always been tall, but with the stick-like long legs of a crane. Now, she could see the large muscle of his thigh being molded by the fabric of dark denim. The jacket draped around her shoulders was expensive and in taking it off he had revealed a crisp white dress shirt, open at the throat. He had on a leather belt that matched the buff of his brown leather shoes.

The sophisticated haircut showed off the lines of his face: the wide intelligent forehead, the straight nose, the extraordinary cheekbones, the full sensual lips.

Lips she had tasted. Kissed. In that one moment that had changed everything.

Had she come here thinking she could put that behind her? That they could just be the best of friends again? Sitting in the tight confines of his car, she just wasn't sure about that, especially since he had matured so exquisitely. The sharp angles of his face had filled in, making him handsome in that extraordinary way that turned heads and elicited smiles from strangers.

At the airport, when she had first caught sight of him, a well-dressed woman—she had had a moment of envy for just how well-dressed the other woman was—had looked at him with interest, bumped him "accidentally" and apologized. How endearing that he'd acknowledged the woman with the briefest nod, hardly glancing up from his phone.

Everything about Oscar—his looks, his clothing, his impeccable grooming, the way he was standing—made him look sophisticated and confident, the man least likely to send an email that said he needed someone.

He had started a company while he was still in university. When she had asked about it, in their infrequent emails, and even more infrequent phone calls, he'd said it was fun and it was doing okay.

What exactly had he said his company was doing? *Saving the world, one piece of garbage at a time*, he'd told her. Recycling. *So* Oscar. And also, so Oscar to downplay his success.

It was obvious, from the car and from the clothing, that he was *very* successful. Nothing in his offhand job description had prepared her for this.

But that was what he came from. Wealth. Stability. Success.

That was what his mother had reminded her all those years ago. That Molly and Oscar came from different worlds and that Molly had no hope of ever fitting into his.

Nastily, his mother, having witnessed their kiss, insinuated Molly might use her body to try to wheedle her way into the Clark world.

I won't allow you to trap him with a tawdry pregnancy, and you don't seem suited to raise a child, period, let alone on your own.

Molly remembered her words now, feeling that same horrendous shame she had felt at the time.

So nearly everything about him was a surprise except the fact he had a plan, which he always did. And except for the fact he was still *Galahad*: the perfect knight, always known for his courage, gentleness, courtesy and chivalry.

Oscar to a T, in other words.

Molly had always made it clear that she was the woman least in need of rescuing. She could look after herself, thank you very much.

And yet his eyes and his smile were so much as she remembered them, and gave her the same feeling. A delicious sense of being at home with someone, comfortable with them, safe, able to relax her defenses.

But the new look and the new physique didn't feel safe at all. Instead, they felt faintly dangerous.

Somehow, she had thought his apartment, a glass-and-steel condo building located close to the ocean, would be more "scientist geek" in its decor: a few experiments on the go, an absent-minded jacket tossed by the door, interesting books scattered about, maybe a gerbil or two in a cage.

But when they took the elevator up, it opened to a corridor with only one front door—his. His space, to her photographer's eye, looked ready for a photo op for Houzz, the home renovation website. Nothing was out of place. Everything was new, and clean, and shiny. The decor, the space, like his clothing and his car, were exquisitely sophisticated, and reflected a level of success she had not known about.

As she surrendered the jacket, Molly reminded herself, this was what he came from. He had grown up in a home very much like this one, beautiful, but faintly impersonal, like the very best of hotel rooms.

She was aware he was watching her.

"What's that look on your face?" he asked quietly.

"It's just not what I expected."

"In what way?"

"It doesn't look like anyone lives here!"

"It doesn't?" he said, looking around with a frown.

"Where are the books about all the millions of things that interest you at any given time? *The Sex Life of Geckos, Secrets of the Volcanoes, Beyond Black Holes.* Where's all that?"

"I'll have to put *The Sex Life of Geckos* on my reading list," he teased her.

Molly hoped it wasn't a Freudian slip that she had mentioned any kind of sex life to him. She decided to deflect.

"Where's the milkshake maker? The popcorn machine? The T-shirt collection? The socks on the floor?"

To her great relief, Oscar tossed the damp jacket carelessly on the couch.

"It probably looked more like that before. When Cynthia and I got engaged, I gave her free rein of the place. I didn't care what it looked like, and she did. And then, as it turned out, she never moved in anyway."

"I'm sorry, Truck." Why would she feel relieved that Cynthia had never lived here?

He lifted a shoulder, but his eyes were sad as they came to rest on her, and then moved away.

"Plus, the housekeeper was here today. I wanted it to look nice for you. She loves to hide my stuff. I'm not sure why she puts away all the appliances. It's not handy."

He wanted it to look nice *for her*. Somehow, that simple statement made her feel a little more relaxed in the opulent space. She looked around. It was very open. The far end of it was completely taken up with a bank of floor-to-ceiling windows that gave an incredible view of the rain-washed nighttime Vancouver skyline, and the ocean beyond that.

Then a movement caught the corner of her eye. Her mouth fell open.

"That's not—"

"One and the same," he said, watching her.

She fell to her knees. The cat marched over to her, and began to meow loudly.

"Protesting your long absence," Oscar said dryly.

"Georgie," she crooned, opening her arms. The cat climbed into them and she buried her face in his fur. He was, as he always had been, the world's ugliest cat. His gray fur was too long in some places, and too short in others. He had a permanent scowl on his face and a tail shaped like a question mark.

But his purr made up for all of his defects. "I can't believe you have him," she whispered. "I wanted to ask, but I think I was scared of the answer. I think your mom only tolerated him for Ralphie. I recall she was furious when I gave him the cat. Apparently there was supposed to be a long consultation process."

At the time, it had seemed like a small—but still sweet—revenge that Mrs. Clark was going to have to tolerate the cat, not quite managing to get rid of everything about Molly.

"I had to track him down to a shelter."

There was something in his tone that suggested he had had words with his mother.

"Thank you," she said softly, "Especially since I don't remember you caring much for him, either."

Oscar. Even though he had never cared for this cat, he was *that* guy. The one you could count on to be decent, no matter what.

"That's not entirely accurate. He hated me. In fact, he hated anyone who wasn't you. Or Ralphie."

Still, Molly had to fight back tears. "But you love him now?" she asked.

Oscar laughed. "That's a little too strong. We tolerate each other."

"And he's with you for good?"

"Of course. He's part of Ralphie. And you."

He acted as if he'd admitted something he hadn't meant to, and went on quickly, "Besides, I'd miss the old guy glaring balefully at me if I don't buy the right brand of cat food. Stalking after me, demanding kitty treats."

With the cat still in her arms, she got to her feet. She felt vulnerable in a way she had not felt since her father died.

Cared about in a way, she realized sadly, she had not felt in about the same length of time. Her hard-earned independence suddenly felt exhausting.

"Is that a pool out there?" she asked as a diversion from the uncomfortable feelings clawing at her throat. It was a pretty good diversion: beautiful, the infinity edge made it look like water was cascading off the side of the building.

"Yeah, and a hot tub."

"Like a common pool and hot tub for the whole building?"

"No," he said. "It belongs to this unit."

His level of arrival took away the sense of coming home that the cat had given her. Georgie still in her arms, purring deeply, she went over and looked at the pool, its turquoise waters twinkling under soft patio lights. The hot tub was separated from the pool by a stone ledge, a waterfall cascading between the two.

"I didn't bring a bathing suit," she said regretfully.

"None required."

She whirled and looked at him, wide-eyed. He gave her a teasing grin. She focused on the living room, feeling a hint of that delicious danger in the air between them.

"Most people who come aren't expecting the pool. I keep a selection of suits in the cabana."

"Oh," she said, pretending grave interest in the room to keep him from seeing her blush. Why was he making her blush so much? They had known each other forever!

Deep distressed leather couches faced each other across a rug that she knew from her travels was Turkish and probably very expensive. At the other end of the room was a sleek kitchen, all stainless steel and granite. An island the approximate size of a billiards table faced the living room.

"This looks like something out of a movie set," she said. Again, it was the not-lived-in look and she found it faintly distressing.

"Which movie?"

"Obviously not *Little House on the Prairie*."

"That wasn't a movie, Mary Ellen."

"You're mixing it up with *The Waltons*. And not like that, either. More like something out of James Bond."

Oscar laughed. "Double-O-Seven at your service."

That was almost worse than picturing him as Galahad!

Still, his laugh reminded her what he was to her, that she didn't need to feel uncomfortable or intimidated by him. She turned back to the room and caught a glimpse of large framed photos on the walls going up a wide hallway. She went and looked at them.

They were hung, and lit, as beautifully as if they were in a gallery.

"They're all mine," she whispered.

He came and stood beside her. "This one's my favorite," he said. Though who the figure in the photo was would not be distinguishable to most people looking at it, they both knew it was a self-portrait of her taken on a timer. She was sitting on a rock ledge, her feet dangling into space, gazing off to the distant peaks.

"Why would this be your favorite?" she asked. "Truck, you're terrified of heights."

"You look so relaxed, despite the fact a sneeze could send you to certain death. I see such strength in it. Independence. Gratitude. Almost every time I look at it, I see something else. It's a great photo, Molly."

She felt the smart of tears, again. Oscar had always had this gift. He saw in her things that others missed, or perhaps things she kept deliberately hidden.

"But every time I look at it, I do think, *how is it she's not scared?*"

She looked at the picture. "You know how some parents come down hard on lying or beating up your brother or stealing cookies before supper? My dad detested fear. It just wasn't tolerated in his world. Some people say, *go big or go home*, but he said, *go bold or go home*. He approved of taking chances, being a daredevil, being courageous. The words I never heard from him were, *be careful*. I think I'm a better person for it."

"You are the bravest person I know."

Well, she thought, except in matters of the heart, where maybe *real* bravery was required. She walked down the wall of photos and stopped at one. This time the tears did come. "This one is my favorite of all time," she whispered, not trusting her voice.

It was true. She had traveled the world, won awards, her photographs were in countless distinguished personal and gallery collections, but this photo, which she had never published, that no one had a print of other than Truck, and her, was her favorite.

Ironically, it was a portrait. She had started seriously taking photos when she was sixteen. She had been accompanying her father on a trip to Africa, where he had been working on a movie. It had been one of his longest jobs he'd ever had and they'd been in Africa for over a year.

He had loved her action shots, and her wildlife shots, but had always been more lukewarm about landscapes and portraits. She wasn't sure whether it was just that she had a natural talent for those things or whether it was because she had adored her father's approval, but she focused her career almost entirely on wildlife now.

But this photo was a black-and-white, a headshot, of Ralphie. He had had Down syndrome and it had been taken right after he was awarded his participant medal in the Special World Games.

Across the bottom of it, scrawled in his childish printing, was Ralphie's motto for life: *Go for it*.

"I love it, too," Oscar said quietly, and his hand came to rest on her shaking shoulders. "It reminds me of such a great time—our senior year, after you got back from Africa, when you and I were assistant coaches on his team."

"I remember it being difficult at times but so worth it," she said with affection through the tears.

"I think it may have been the happiest time of my whole life," Oscar said quietly.

She absorbed that. Here was a man who had achieved phenomenal success and yet that time with his brother remained his happiest.

And hers, now that she thought about it. The cat's purr deepened as if it were satisfied that she had recognized a basic truth.

"And you captured it," Oscar said. "You captured our moment in time. Because the look on his face says it all. What I love best about the photo is it doesn't even show the medal, and yet the triumph is so evident. That's how I felt about his life. The joy of him overshadowed everything else. He triumphed over incredible challenges. I miss him so much."

He handed her a hankie. So Oscar! Who else would have a beautiful linen hankie available for moments like this?

Molly dabbed at her eyes. She hated crying. It was weak. "I would have come if there had been a service."

"I know. It wasn't my choice to make."

Molly heard a trace of anger in his voice that reflected her own. His mother had made the choices, of course, as was a parent's right. But it had only underscored Molly's uncomfortable feeling that Ralphie had disrupted the perfect picture Mrs. Clark wanted of her family to show the world.

Instead of the service, Mrs. Clark's choice

had been to put Ralphie's name on a swim pavilion being constructed in his honor. It was a huge gesture but, to Molly, as a way to commemorate Ralphie's life, it lacked heart.

"Ever since you mentioned it, I've been mulling over an idea to honor him," Molly said.

"Have you come up with something?"

"I think so. But that's my secret. Will you trust me with it?"

The relief on his face reminded her of why she had come. For once, Oscar needed her, and it felt of grave importance to be able to do this for him.

"Of course," he said quietly. "He loved you so much, Molly. He treasured every postcard and every photo you ever sent him. After you would video chat with him, he would call me and give me the highlights. And all I would hear is how Molly had seen an elephant. A real elephant. A real elephant with a baby. A real elephant with a baby in Africa."

The tears came again, and Oscar's arms folded around her, squishing Georgie deeper into her breast. Oscar smelled so good. He felt so strong. She wanted to melt into that embrace and let him hold her forever.

But forever was not in her vocabulary and never had been. And she certainly wasn't going to risk one of the most important things in her world—her friendship with this man—by changing anything about their relationship now.

Even though it felt so tempting here in the circle of his arms, feeling the steady beat of his heart under the softness of her cheek, inhaling the intoxicating clean man scent of him. She could not make herself push away.

It was Georgie's howl of protest that made them let go of each other. She gave Oscar a watery smile.

"You know it isn't like me to be teary. I think I might be more jet-lagged than I thought. Can you show me where to freshen up?"

"Sure, I'll show you your room."

"How should I dress for the surprise?"

He laughed, and again his laughter deepened her sense of being comfortable—even giving in to tears—in this space that was so posh.

"The surprise is here, so anything you want from pajamas to an evening gown."

"Yeah," she said wryly. "I packed that. An evening gown. I think my Versace. And my pearls."

The strangest thing was, ever so briefly, she wished she did have a Versace and pearls, just to try it, just to see…

"Pajamas it is."

"How do you know I don't have pajamas that would make you completely uncomfortable if I trotted out in them?" she demanded.

He looked at her. He smiled. "Because you haven't changed a bit."

"Hey! Do I have to remind you I've become a high commodity item in the photography world?"

"That doesn't mean you've changed," he said, with soft certainty. "That means others have been allowed to see what I always saw."

CHAPTER FOUR

SHEESH! MOLLY FELT as if Oscar was going to make her cry again if he kept it up. But he deliberately changed to a lighter tone of voice.

"I bet Molly Bentwell, world's most-sought-after photographer, still wears boy bottoms in some shade of plaid and a T-shirt for pajamas."

It was true. She wore the same kind of pajamas she had always worn. Why had she become predictable, when he had not? Why did she suddenly long for something a little more delicate, more feminine? She'd like to see a look of shock—and maybe appreciation—on his face.

He knew what kind of pajamas Molly wore because he used to call at her window, and she would climb out of it, and they would lay on her roof in the dark of night.

He would name all the constellations. He could tell her how many light years away Mars—that little red speck in the sky—was.

He could explain dark holes and the big bang theory with such ease.

Good grief. A pajama party with her best friend. She didn't know if she was disappointed in the surprise or thrilled by it. Or faintly frightened. Because it might be true that she had not changed all that much.

But he had.

Oscar had no remnants of the boy he had once been remaining in him. He was 100 percent potent and powerful man.

"What are you wearing?" she asked him. "Your pajamas?"

He lifted his eyebrow at her in a way that stole her breath—and suggested he didn't wear pajamas!

He carried her bag down a wide hallway and set it, with extra care, inside a bedroom door. The fact that he remembered her cameras were in there reminded her of why he was that guy— the one who could be counted on to always do the right thing, in big ways and small.

She shut the door behind her and put the cat on the bed. Georgie curled up, and made it seem a bit more relaxed, almost homey, thank goodness. Because the room was gorgeous: deep luxurious carpet, the bed covered in layers of soft gray fabrics, the walls papered in a subtly patterned silk, a wall-to-ceiling window looking over the glorious city and ocean view. It had all the personality of a hotel room, which made her wonder about Cynthia.

Which was none of her business!

It had its own bathroom, and Molly dragged her bag in and tossed off her travel-rumpled clothes. Gratefully, she got into the shower.

When she got out, she was sorry she had thrown only her normal travel kit into her bag, not that anything she had left at home was that exciting, either. What was it about Oscar that was making her want to explore a different side of herself?

She laid out everything she had brought with her: one pair of stretchy black pants that could look formal in a pinch. One tailored white shirt. One tailored striped shirt. One pair of ballet-style shoes. The khakis she had just taken off, which she would rinse out tonight. Three T-shirts. A pair of casual shoes. Enough comfortable underwear for three days before she'd have to start washing it. A sturdy pair of light boots that would go well with the khakis. One pair of pajamas: no surprise, plaid bottoms and any one of the T-shirts she had brought.

Molly considered the stretchy black pants and the white shirt, but they really weren't any more alluring than her pajamas.

Alluring? With Truck? She put on her pajamas, and she put them on hastily.

She took a deep breath and walked out of her room. The cat woke from his snooze, jumped off the bed and followed her, as always, dog-like in his devotion.

Oscar was in the kitchen. Now it looked as if someone lived here. He had a variety of ingredients spread out around him. He was in a black chef's apron and chopping something with a sharp knife with amazing speed and comfort. Molly lived a life of fast food, grabbing bites to eat when she had time.

Seeing Oscar so at home in his amazing kitchen should have been sweet and made her feel more comfortable. Instead, she found it disconcertingly sexy.

"You look like a professional chef," she said.

"And you put on your pajamas. I'm glad. I want you to be comfortable."

He didn't tease her that he'd been right about her pajama selection, just grinned at her, and it made everything, including her choice of what to wear, seem just right.

"This is the surprise," he said, pleased. "I cook. Are you impressed?"

"I guess that will depend how good you are at it," she teased him.

"Oh, I'm good. It goes surprisingly well with

a science background. It *is* science, really. Pellegrino Artusi recognized that in 1891."

Who dropped names from 1891? Oscar. *Her Truck.*

"Can I do something?" she asked.

"No, tonight I'm looking after you."

I'm looking after you. It felt like a weakness to enjoy those words so much.

"What are we having?" She went and glanced at what he was preparing. She laughed. "Hamburgers, Chef Oscar?"

"I'm saving the big culinary reveal for tomorrow. Tonight, I tried to think what you might miss about home. I decided a person could only eat so much bratwurst and spaetzle before they started craving a big one hundred percent Canadian beef burger. I'm going to grill for you."

There it was again. *For you.* His thoughtfulness was in such sharp contrast to every man she had ever tried to have a relationship with that Molly felt faintly squishy inside.

Weak.

She tried to kid it away. "I'm a vegetarian," she announced.

He glanced at her. And saw right through her. "Nice try. Here. You can do one thing. Grab that platter and bring it outside."

"It's raining out."

"It's always raining here," Oscar said. "I've designed the patio to accommodate it."

He filled his own arms with platters and led the way outside. He held open the door for her, and Molly passed through it. Georgie just managed to squeak through, with an indignant meow, before Oscar slid the door shut again.

From inside, Molly had been able to see the pool and hot tub. Now, she saw the outdoor area extended far beyond what was visible from the living room window. Oscar flicked a light and the area was softly illuminated from several sources, including strings of small round bulbs, and a chandelier at the center of the pavilion. Unlike the inside space, there was something about this one that felt warm and cozy and welcoming.

She stood for a moment with her mouth open. "Don't get wet," he said. "Follow Georgie."

The cat obviously had no intention of getting wet. Tail up, he marched over to the outdoor pavilion. Under that large structure was a full stainless steel kitchen that included a huge grill, a fridge and a bar. Beside the food-prep area was furniture like she had never seen. A dining table, with deeply padded chairs, cushioned in tropical lime green leaf pattern, invited people to sit and seemed to promise lively conversation.

He could host a dinner party for at least a dozen people out here! Oscar hosted dinner parties?

There was a huge sectional sofa, and again it was a surprising pop of lime green on the accent cushions that made it seem like the unexpected would happen here. But the most astonishing piece of furniture was a suspended basket chair. Shaped like a teardrop, it looked something like a bird cage with the door taken off. Inside was a nest, created by a huge cushion in that same shade of lime. It was definitely a snuggle spot for two people!

Oscar was watching her. She was drawn to the chair.

"I've never seen anything like this."

Georgie jumped up and made himself at home.

"Try it," Oscar invited her, setting down his platters and walking over to take hers from her. "Hop in."

Molly gave herself over to the chair.

"Oh," she said. Georgie shifted to accommodate her. The chair enveloped her, and swung gently. The cat found his way to her tummy. "It's amazing."

Oscar grinned and bowed. "This is what I do. This is my recycling business."

"Sorry? I'm not following you."

He had a pair of barbecue tongs in his hand. He gestured around—the pagoda, the beautiful furniture inside of it, the chair she was sitting in.

"I recycle waste into this. My company is called Current Ocean. We started with plastics from the ocean, making small items, like necklaces, bracelets and earrings. But we've expanded since. We use a lot of tires now, too. The outdoor furniture has become our major product. It's all completely weatherproof."

"It's incredible." No wonder this space was so warm and welcoming. Unlike this inside space, this was pure Oscar. He had created all of it. She loved that he glowed under her approval.

"Our motto," Oscar told her, "is *making problems into solutions.*"

She almost blurted out that she needed him in her personal life, but what problems did she have? Professionally, her every dream had come true. But personally? She couldn't seem to stay in one place. She couldn't seem to sustain a relationship. She sometimes had this secret longing to be girlie: to get her nails done, to wear high heels, to buy a gorgeous dress, and she fought it off as if it were the worst kind of betrayal of everything she had learned growing up.

He turned and busied himself with the food as she swung gently, watching him, and feeling faintly guilty about it.

"I'm not used to being a lady of leisure. Do you need help?" she asked, as she watched him fire up the grill.

"I told you, I'm looking after you tonight. You've been traveling all day. Relax. Any preferences for music?"

"Metal," she said.

"What kind of vegetarian listens to metal? Hey, Siri, play my list."

Just like that, the space filled with music. The first piece was classical guitar.

Once she would have known what he listened to. The guitar music was the most pleasant of surprises, and so perfect with the setting.

After the first few minutes, she allowed herself to enjoy the sense of being looked after. In her pajamas, snuggled up with the cat, watching Oscar work his magic at the grill, Molly let the incredible smells envelop her and listened to the rain patter on the roof mingling with the selection of music that ranged from flute solos to soft rock and pop.

"Did you drift off?"

Molly opened her eyes, startled. "I didn't think so. I was just so relaxed." She didn't add it had been a long, long time since she had felt that way. Her life always seemed to hum with a fine tension, with the potential for catastrophe to unfold unexpectedly.

It was such a treat to experience this kind of serenity.

"Dinner's ready."

"I'll get up."

"No, you won't. Just shift over. Get rid of the cat."

She saw now Oscar had two plates. She tried to push the cat off, but with a miffed expression, he just moved to the bottom of the cushion.

The chair swung gently as Oscar joined her. It held them both easily, but tightly, touching the full length of their bodies, shoulder to thigh. The feeling of serenity was edged out slightly by the awareness of him—his strength, his scent, his closeness.

He passed a plate to her. She bit into her hamburger.

"Ambrosia," she decided. "And no tomatoes."

"Did you think I'd forget you don't like tomatoes?"

It was a lovely reminder of just how well they knew each other. She didn't like tomatoes. He didn't like pickles. She liked hot sauce. He liked mayo.

But now, seeing him in his lush surroundings, there was a whole part of him she didn't know about, and she wanted to fill in the blanks.

"Tell me more about your business," she invited him.

It turned out Oscar had been earning a degree in chemical engineering, but it was a beach holiday in Thailand where he had first started mulling over the idea of turning plastic, harvested from polluted oceans, into usable objects.

As always, when he talked about science, he became very animated. Over the next years, while still a student, he had tried experiments that succeeded and just as many that failed, but he had finally come up with a formula where he could turn a small amount of plastic into a usable product at a decent price. He had started by making a small necklace.

But it was when he was approached by a furniture designer that things went big. The designer had connections, and with Oscar's business background from his family, Current Ocean exploded. Their products were now in demand around the world.

"I still like being in the lab the best," he admitted. "And as we've grown more successful, I've been able to pull back from the parts I don't like more and more. Cynthia liked the glamorous part of starting an exciting new company: schmoozing, getting invited to important events, but I just didn't care. It was one of many differences between us."

"What happened between you and Cynthia?" Molly realized it was way too personal. Sharing the chair had lulled her into thinking they were best friends, confidants, just as they had been most of their lives. But six years separated them, and a lot of life had passed under the bridge since then.

He hesitated, and then said, his voice low, "You know how you said the apartment looked like no one lived there?"

She nodded.

"The relationship felt the same way. It looked so perfect and felt so…" His voice drifted off. "Don't get me wrong. She's a really great person. We've remained friends. We just discovered we weren't right for each other."

It was so like Oscar to remain friends with an ex. He was such a decent person. But it sounded as if Cynthia had been, too. Why did Molly want to hate her?

"I knew she must be a good person," she said grudgingly. "Ralphie mentioned her sometimes. He liked her."

Something tightened marginally around Oscar's mouth. "That's enough about me. What happened to your last relationship? A musician, right?"

"I suck at relationships," she said, trying to sound breezy, not a hint of finding-someone-else's-panties-under-her-bed in the tone. "It's my lifestyle. I'm never around."

That had been Werner's excuse, too. As if it were somehow her fault he had strayed.

And maybe it had been. Not so much because of lifestyle but because of fear. Fear that she didn't have what it took to make things work out. That she always held part of herself back because love was, as her father had always said, the biggest pain of all.

Look at how she had felt when she left Oscar to go to photography school. Bereft. Between leaving him and losing her father in such a short period of time, she hadn't eaten or slept properly for months. Only the work removed her from the pain, and she had poured herself into it. People thought she had talent, but what she had was a single-minded focus driven by the need to escape the fact she was so alone in the world.

"Are you lonely?" he asked her quietly, always able to read her so accurately.

It was too personal, just like her asking him about Cynthia.

"I don't feel lonely when I work—which is

almost always—I feel alive." Sometimes it was the *only* time she felt fully alive, but she didn't feel ready to surrender that truth to Oscar.

"You take some big chances to get those photos," he said quietly. "Is that what makes you feel alive? The adrenaline rush of surviving?"

"I *like* being death-defying," she said stubbornly. "It's in my blood."

Did she feel Oscar shudder ever so slightly beside her?

"I hear a *but* there."

Shoot. She'd never been able to hide her truth from him. She tried, anyway. "No, you don't."

"Yes, I do."

He was her best friend. Was he still? It felt like it. She was shocked that she wanted to tell someone.

"Sometimes I look at a normal couple in the park with a Golden Retriever and a baby on a blanket and I itch to capture that baby with my camera, instead of a pride of lions lunching on a gazelle or a hippo crushing a canoe in his jaws."

"So, do that," he said, as if it were the easiest choice in the world.

"You know what babies lead to?"

"Is this a trick question? I know what leads to babies."

She could feel herself blush. She gave him a little warning nudge with her fist. There were certain conversations that were not going to be safe for them. What led to babies was going to be one of those.

"Weddings," she said, glumly. "Babies lead to weddings."

"Um, I think you might have that backward. I thought weddings led to babies. As hopelessly old-fashioned as that makes me."

She shot him a look. She *loved* that about him. That he was hopelessly old-fashioned, a traditional kind of guy. Honorable. Decent.

"Photography," she said. "Baby photos lead to wedding photos. I've already had several requests. I *hate* wedding photos."

"But you'd like to do baby photos," he said, too astute, as always.

She was silent for a long time. "Can you keep a secret?"

"You've always been able to tell me your secrets," he reminded her.

"I've regretted it, too."

"You have not!"

"Remember the time I told you I had a crush on Vincent Marcello?"

"We were thirteen!"

"Aha! So, you do remember."

"Okay, yes I do."

"And then a week after I confided in you, he asked me if I wanted to go to a movie with him. I always wondered if that was a coincidence."

"I don't recall the details."

"Did you tell him?"

"Of course not. I might have hinted that if he asked you out, you'd say yes. That wasn't giving away your secret. It was using something I knew about you to make your dreams come true."

"He might have asked me out on his own."

"I doubt that. All the guys were scared to ask you out."

"How come? My dad?"

"Well, maybe that, a bit, but mostly you'd beaten them all at arm wrestles."

"Anyway, all your efforts did not make my dreams come true," Molly said. "He turned out not to be a white knight."

"Thirteen is a little early to want to be whisked off on a white charger, anyway."

"He tried to kiss me in the theater without my permission. I blacked his eye."

Oscar chuckled softly. "And sealed your dating fate for the rest of your school years."

"I never really believed in that white-knight stuff, anyway."

"But you wanted to," Oscar said softly.

This was the problem with being with a person who knew you so well, knew you better, sometimes, than you knew yourself. This was the problem with someone knowing your secrets and wanting to help your dreams come true.

"Well," Molly said, after an uncomfortable silence between them, "I'm even more jaundiced now than Vincent Marcello left me."

"I know," Oscar said, quietly, his voice threaded through with sympathy. "But there's been some winners along the way, hasn't there?"

"I'm having a nice night. I don't want to talk about it."

"Okay, let's get back to your secret, then."

She hesitated. "I think I'd like to do more portraits," she admitted.

He actually chuckled. "That's the big secret?"

But that was only part of it. The other part she would never tell him because she could barely admit it to herself. Seeing families, wanting to photograph them, to capture what they had, seemed to be about some secret yearning in herself. A yearning for belonging. For warmth. For hope. That secret was, well, terrifying.

The fact that she longed for the thing her father had detested the most—normalcy—felt like some kind of betrayal.

"That's it," she said. "That's the big secret."

"Have to say I don't get it. Who would pick taking a picture of a baby instead of standing in front of a charging bull elephant, having it blow snot in your face?" he teased her.

"The elephant snot thing was only once."

"It was Ralphie's favorite story from you," he told her, with a smile.

"You don't get it," she said dismissively. "I love the challenge of getting a great shot. Anybody with a bubble blower and a teddy bear can get a great shot of a baby."

CHAPTER FIVE

THE PROBLEM, OSCAR THOUGHT, with Molly in her pajamas, nestled under his arm, the rain pattering on the pagoda roof, the soft music and the cat at their feet, was not that he didn't get it.

The problem was that he got it completely.

He'd always gotten it.

This was a part of Molly that she did not show the world. Despite that image she loved—the fearless photographer facing down the charging elephant—Molly yearned for all the things everyone yearned for. Family. Connection. Children.

But she saw those yearnings as a weakness. As things to be kept secret.

He got up and got them both a glass of wine, then returned to the chair. It was, as it had always been, just so easy to be with Molly. Their conversation roamed easily between old friends and new interests, current events and the hometown changes.

But there was a new element there, too. An element he had introduced, six years ago, the last time he had seen her.

He'd kissed her.

Thoroughly.

And it was not the kind of thing a man just put out of his head, especially with her fitting so comfortably against him again now.

Like they were two pieces of a puzzle made to fit together precisely.

The chill of the rainy night began to gather around them, but instead of suggesting they go in, he went and got a blanket, and lit the ethanol fireplace. He refilled their wine glasses and came back to the chair.

He covered them both with the blanket.

"It reminds me of the old days," she said, "sitting on the roof outside my bedroom window together. We used to talk until our voices were hoarse. Remember?"

Of course, he remembered.

And that's what they did again now. They talked until their voices were hoarse, and they couldn't keep their eyes open another second, and then they fell asleep, cocooned from the world, not just by the chair but by each other.

Her breathing had grown deep and steady, when suddenly she jerked. And then she sat up.

"Oh, geez," she said, "I've forgotten to check

my messages. I'm waiting for a really important call."

Oscar felt the disappointment of this moment coming to an end. Of her other world infringing. But he recognized, ultimately, it was for the best.

"It's late here, anyway," he said, getting up from the chair, and reaching out a hand to help her. "I was getting ready to turn in."

That wasn't true. He had been getting ready to stay up all night—or to fall asleep in the big chair with her. Whatever happened.

But that was over now. Molly let go of his hand as soon as she was out of the chair and scrambled through the rain to the door. The cat gave him a look that said, *See? She's mine*, and then jumped off the chair and followed her.

Oscar gathered the dishes and food, double-checked that the barbecue was off and went into the apartment.

Molly was sprawled on the couch inside, going through her phone with an intense look on her face. She looked somehow right in his space, bringing it the thing it had never had, and that she had sensed it was lacking right away.

Life.

As he watched, the scowl left her face. She

beamed down at the screen. The look on her face—anticipation, delight—made him wonder who she had just heard from. Was it a man that brought that look to her face? She had just extradited herself from one of her horrible choices. Surely, she wasn't already—

None of his business, he told himself firmly. It was probably work. Work was, by her own admission, the thing that made her feel alive. He was aware he wanted other things to make her feel alive, but that made him look at her lips.

And recall feeling as alive as he had ever felt. But that was about him. Because whatever she had felt that night they had kissed had been part of what had driven her away.

Friends. They were just friends. Despite his niggling awareness of her—or maybe because of it—it was his responsibility to keep it that way.

She looked up at him. The glow from whatever she had seen on that phone still showing on her face.

"Thank you for a wonderful night, Oscar." She got up off the couch, came and stood before him, reached up on her tiptoes and pecked his cheek. "I've got some stuff I have to look after."

And then she was gone. Her bedroom door clicked shut behind her.

Oscar resisted the impulse to lay his fingers across his cheek where her lips had touched. He went to his room, shut the door, shucked off his clothes and slid between the sheets. On second thought, he could not imagine being in the same apartment with her and having no clothes on.

Annoyed with himself, he got up and rummaged through a drawer until he found something that resembled pajama bottoms. Something like what she would wear.

He got back into bed, contemplating the strange, irrational restlessness he felt. Nothing had happened, really. They'd had dinner, visited, fallen asleep. The cat had thrown him over for her, completely, and Molly had shared a few harmless secrets.

Nothing had happened.

And yet it felt as if a wind were picking up, tossing a few items of his life around. Really, wasn't that restless feeling the first warning that a tornado was about to strike?

She was, Oscar reminded himself firmly, his oldest friend. They had known each other since they were five years old.

He knew her better than he knew any other living soul on earth.

And yet, when he thought of that long-ago moment, when their lips had touched, he was aware something had changed between them that could not be put back the way it was before.

In some ways, Molly felt like a stranger to him now.

Like he didn't know her at all anymore.

Yes, it felt like there was a tornado coming. He would just have to make sure to batten down the hatches. And avoid the worst of the storm.

He was glad he had a nice safe bike ride planned for tomorrow.

Oscar was shaken out of his spiraling thoughts by a muffled sound. It was her phone ringing. He willed her to ignore it. He willed her to be glaring at it.

But no, she answered.

Oscar was ashamed to strain his ears, listening. Breathless.

Hello, James.

Oscar pulled the pillow over his head. And then, even more ashamed of himself, took it off and listened some more. Just long enough to hear her laugh and say something about how she never wore dresses. Which was true.

Except now, if he was hearing correctly, she was promising to wear one for James. He put in his ear buds. He told himself he was not jealous. There was no way he was jealous. He was feeling protective of her, that was all. She did have a tendency to jump into things with both feet. In Molly's world, regret was for later.

He was up early the next morning and felt as if he had not slept a wink. Grumpily, he threw a robe over his pajama bottoms and padded out to the kitchen.

Molly appeared a few minutes later, looking annoyingly giddy, as if she had experienced a fantastic sleep.

"Look," she said gleefully, pointing at him, "matching pajamas."

"Huh," he said.

"I thought—" She stopped herself in the nick of time. She was blushing, though. It pleased him in some wicked way that she was blushing, thinking of him naked while she was planning on wearing a dress for James.

"You look tired," she said to him.

"Do I? I'm not a morning person."

She cocked her head at him as if her lie detector was beeping.

"I'm not sure what we should get up to today," he said. "I was planning a bike ride, but look at the weather."

Molly went and looked out the window. "I love bike riding in the rain," she said.

"You would," he said.

* * *

An hour later, he found himself in a little store close to Stanley Park, waiting while Molly tried on raincoats.

And galoshes.

"I wonder if they have this in any other color than yellow?" she said, wrinkling her nose at the coat. "I don't like yellow."

"Who doesn't like a whole color?" he asked her, still feeling unreasonably crabby with her, especially with her standing there looking so utterly adorable.

"Who doesn't like a whole time of day?" she shot back. "'When you arise in the morning, think of what a precious privilege it is to be alive, to breathe, to think, to enjoy, to love.' That's Marcus Aurelius."

"'Yellow,'" he shot back, "'excites a warm and agreeable impression... The eye is gladdened, the heart expanded and cheered, a glow seems at once to breathe toward us.' That's von Goethe."

She considered. "My Aurelius trumps your von Goethe."

"How come you get to decide that?"

And then they were laughing at how quickly this old game had come back to them and Oscar felt some tension he had been holding in himself slide away. She bought the yellow jacket and the rubber boots.

* * *

Molly had awoken in the morning to find several more messages on her phone. Her plans were coming together so well for Ralphie's memorial event that she felt nearly giddy with it.

Or maybe that was a lie to herself. All that giddiness could be from spending a lovely evening cuddled up with Truck… She went out into the apartment, trying to tell herself she wasn't feeling what she was feeling.

But she'd felt excited to see him.

However, it was quickly apparent that he didn't share her feelings. Oscar was downright grumpy. He said he wasn't a morning person, but she didn't remember that about him. If she didn't know better, she'd guess he had a hangover.

He was making coffee, and had a selection of pastries out for breakfast. He had on a very posh robe, like the kind you got in expensive hotels, and he looked very sleep mussed and sexy. His stubble had thickened overnight and it was quite a roguish look. She had felt a funny little desire to touch his face and see what it felt like.

She was aware he didn't look as giddy as she felt. But after they had the little quote battle, whatever tension had been there seemed to ease off.

Molly was thrilled to find, because of the rain, they had the famed Stanley Park seawall mostly to themselves. With Oscar slightly behind her, she aimed at a puddle. She hit it full force and the water sprayed out behind her. She looked over her shoulder and laughed gleefully at his expression when the water sprayed him.

That old competitiveness leaped up between them and he raced by her. She tried to slow down, but wasn't quick enough. He shifted in front of her and she saw the puddle he was aiming for way too late for her to avoid it.

"Bombs away," he shouted, and a wave of muddy water cascaded over her.

"Oh, yeah? Watch this." She tried to pull out to pass him. He blocked her. She tried the other side. He blocked her again. She finally managed to squeeze beside him, and they raced side by side, like two Thoroughbreds heading for the finish line. Their breathless shouts of laughter filled the air. She saw a jogger coming. One of them was going to have to move or they'd be playing chicken with the poor jogger.

As she had known he would, Oscar—ever the gentleman—reluctantly swung in behind her. She looked for a puddle. She chortled with glee when she saw the one coming. It was enormous. A lake! He was going to get soaked to the skin.

She aimed right for it. She peddled hard and lifted her feet high in the air as the water grabbed her tires. She glanced behind her.

Oscar had stopped, and was leaning on his handlebars, grinning. She realized she shouldn't have looked back. The handlebars wobbled in the deep water. The tire wallowed. The bike abruptly slowed and veered left.

Her pant legs snagged on the bike as it started to fall over. She came off with an ungracious plop and the bike fell on top of her. She heard a tearing sound, and then the water closed over her head.

She emerged from the puddle laughing, sputtering and spitting out water, to find Oscar had abandoned his bike and was kneeling, heedless of the water, in the puddle beside her.

"Are you okay?"

She looked at the concern on his face. His glasses were covered in water from mud puddles and the rain. He hadn't shaved this morning, and little droplets of water clung to his stubble.

Something in her went very weak. She *wanted* him to pick her up, and carry her over to the grass, and tenderly touch the place on her ankle where it hurt. And she wanted to touch that damned attractive stubble!

Instead, she splashed him, got out of the puddle and raced for her bike.

"Hey," he called after her, "just an FYI, you're showing the whole world your panties."

CHAPTER SIX

IT HAS BEEN such a long and wonderful day. They had spent most of it on the bikes, exploring Stanley Park, playful and then sedate. Oscar had given Molly his jacket to tie around her exposed behind. When she'd objected, he had said he couldn't get any wetter, which was certainly true. Finally, soaked to shivering, they had headed back to his place.

Despite her jet-lag strategy, Molly had come out of the shower and told herself she would just lie down for a minute. When she woke up, she could hear Oscar in the kitchen, and something already smelled good.

Because of the ripped pants, she had only two choices left to wear, so she went with the stretchy black pants and white shirt tonight instead of her pajamas.

"Come on over," Oscar said, when she came down the hall. "I have a job for you."

He was freshly showered and changed. He

was wearing the chef's apron over his clothes again, and she noticed he had shaved, finally. She wanted to touch his freshly shaven face the same way she had wanted to touch his stubble.

"A job for me?" she said, joining him at the island, ordering herself to focus on the task at hand. Unfortunately, the fresh scent that came off him was heady and masculine, and as good as whatever was cooking in the oven. And even more distracting.

"Oh, Truck," she warned him, "you know my culinary skill runs to boiling an egg, right?"

"Right," he said. "I've already taken that under consideration."

"Chefs are notoriously bad-tempered and temperamental," she informed him.

"This, to the man who rescued you from the mud puddle," he said, aghast. "Who gave you his jacket to prevent your derriere from becoming public knowledge, who tried three different ice-cream places before we found one with licorice flavor."

"Okay, okay."

"Having said that—" he wagged his knife at her "—do exactly as I tell you, and nothing else."

"Yes, Chef," she said with pretend meekness, and they both laughed at the impossibility of her ever being meek.

He held out an apron, and he slipped it over her head, and she turned and let him tie it behind her back.

His hands brushed the small of her back. His breath touched the nape of her neck. It was strangely and sumptuously intimate.

Molly didn't think of Truck like this! Except that she had been, all day, starting with his stubble.

"What are you making?" she asked, turning quickly to look at the counter top.

"A dish I looked up on the internet. It's called How to Impress a Girl."

"That doesn't sound very scientific." She gulped when she realized what he had said. "Are you trying to impress me?"

"I don't have to, do I?"

"No, of course not." She recovered quickly. "But I can see it's a good idea for you to practice. For when you do. Want to impress a girl, that is."

How wrong was it to have the dangerous wish that she were that girl? Today had been so much fun. What would it be like to have a life like that?

"That's going to be never," he said, firmly. "I've decided I'm forever single."

"Me, too," she said.

"Ha."

"What does that mean?"

"It doesn't take a psychology major to figure out there's something behind that secret longing to take baby pictures."

Her mouth opened. Then snapped shut. Sometimes that was the problem with having a best friend. They saw things too clearly.

"Here," he said, deftly changing the subject. "Open the pomegranate."

"Who cooks with a pomegranate?" Molly groused, looking at the hard pinkish cylinder-shaped fruit he had placed in her hand.

"We're not cooking with it. It's going in the salad." Oscar put a small sharp paring knife in front of her.

She glared at the pomegranate, the knife and him. "I don't know how to open a pomegranate."

It was an unexpected reminder that this was his world: where people knew how to open pomegranates. She bet his mother knew how. And Cynthia.

"For Pete's sake, Molly, it's not a test of your worthiness. We're supposed to have fun."

Again, that reminder that Oscar knew her so well, and could see things others missed. Despite professional recognition, she still sometimes felt like that girl who was not good enough.

"Anyone who can take photos like you does not have to be a domestic diva," Oscar told her firmly, fishing his phone out from under that sexy apron. "It's not rocket science. Here. Look it up."

"Domestic diva-ing?"

"Pomegranate opening!" He was busy finely chopping herbs and the rich aroma of rosemary joined the other scents in the air.

She found his phone in her hands. His screen saver was her photo of Ralphie.

"Hey," she said, scrolling through his phone. "Did you know every pomegranate is supposed to have exactly six hundred and thirteen seeds? Wow. It's biblical or something. We should count them."

"Even I am not that scientific of a scientist," he said. "Are you done opening that thing yet?"

He was grating cheese.

"The pomegranate," she continued, "is revered for its beauty, flowers and fruit. It symbolizes sanctity, fertility and abundance."

Thankfully, he turned from her just then, placing a tray of bread rolls with cheese and rosemary sprinkled on them in the oven. She couldn't possibly be blushing because she had said the word *fertility* in his presence!

"Were you and Cynthia going to have kids?" she asked.

"Did you know you have the attention span of a gnat?" he growled at her, coming to stand behind her, and looking over her shoulder at the pomegranate.

"You're being very disapproving," she said. "I knew I wouldn't like you with a chef's temperament!"

"In my defense, I'd like to eat sometime before midnight."

"Okay, okay." She watched a two-minute video on sectioning a pomegranate. In the video, the correctly sectioned fruit fell open like a flower, and then the seeds could be easily scooped from it. "Were you?"

"Wanting to eat before midnight?" he asked dryly.

"Wanting to have children."

"Were you and your latest?" he shot back.

"I asked first." She held her breath and cut into the pomegranate. Bright red juice sprayed out of it, splattering on the cuff of her white shirt.

"Yeah," he said gruffly. We planned on having kids someday."

Oscar—her Truck—had contemplated having a child with a woman…who was not her. Molly and Oscar were *friends*. She hadn't even seen him for six years. She knew he had been engaged. So why did it feel, oddly, like a betrayal?

Probably because being here with him made him so *real* for her, all over again, as if six years hadn't separated them.

"Were you?" he asked. He had moved away. His tone was casual, but he wasn't looking at her. "Going to have a child? Some day? Does longing to take baby pictures mean something?"

What could she say to that? *I don't pick the kind of men anyone sane would ever have children with. On purpose. Because your mother told me I didn't seem suited to raise a child.*

She slid him a look. He was looking at her now, reading her face for the clues that only he would see. And she did not want him to see this one: Oscar was the kind of man a woman picked if she wanted to have children. Infinitely stable. Mature enough to put the needs of another human being ahead of his own.

He was the kind of guy you wanted in your baby pictures.

Not that she ever wanted to think about Oscar like that.

"My lifestyle doesn't give itself to having children," she said carefully. "I can't even keep a plant alive. I even abandoned poor Georgie."

"Not really abandoned. Ralphie loved him

as much as you did. I always thought I'd have kids," he said softly. "Until Ralphie died. Something changed in me. Cynthia saw it."

Molly looked at him. Nothing had changed in him. Oscar had always been *that* guy. The one with deep loyalties. The one who wanted to protect everything he loved. The one who was stable. The one who had an instinct for the right thing. It told her more about Cynthia than about him, that his betrothed had not understood his struggle with the death of his brother, the depth of his grief, the unending sea that would be his sorrow. How could anyone know him and not know he would take the death of someone he loved as an affront to his need for order and control and predictability?

"She didn't deserve you," she said simply.

He lifted a shoulder. "There was something missing, even before Ralphie died. She knew it. I knew it. We just couldn't put our finger on it."

Passion, Molly thought, and was stunned at herself. She didn't really know anything about Cynthia.

Except that she'd seen a picture or two of her, in her designer clothes, and diamond tennis bracelets, her perfect makeup and hair. She'd seen this apartment.

"Ah, look, Molly, you've gone and massacred the pomegranate."

She looked down. The pomegranate was in a messy heap in front of her. The bright ruby red juice had not only stained the cuff of her shirt but also her hands and the countertop. The precious little seeds—that stood for fertility— were mashed in with the pulp in a pretty much unsalvageable mess.

For some reason, the destruction of the pomegranate—or maybe the fact Oscar had not been loved passionately, the way he deserved to be loved—made her want to cry.

"I've ruined my shirt," she said, her voice wobbly. She didn't like wobbliness, and she was miffed at herself that she was experiencing quite a bit of it since landing in Vancouver.

However, if it had to come out, she was glad it was with him. She was pretty sure Oscar was the only person in the whole world she ever trusted with this side of herself. Not the fearless photographer, but the side that wobbled every now and then.

He was looking at her so intently. As if he knew darn well it wasn't about a shirt. She realized she had missed seeing his eyes: the intensity of his gaze, the intelligence, the compassion.

"We'll get you a new one," he said, going along with her claim it was about the shirt. "There's some of the best shopping in the world here."

Normally, she would have reminded him she hated shopping. But suddenly, she *wanted* to shop. To find something new. Maybe to let loose a side of herself she had never dared explore.

"Okay," she said.

"Well, that was the surprise answer," he said with a grin.

That grin—lopsided, boyish, charming— drew her back to their simple days together, filled with friendship and laughter. Days when maybe she had dared to hold the secret hope— even as she proclaimed her independence, her utter lack of *need*—that she would have a normal life and a normal family, despite the fact she had not been raised to see that as a worthy goal.

Don't fall into the trap of security, her father had always instructed her. *Adventure is the elixir of life.*

And fall into the trap she hadn't. And yet the pursuit of adventure had left her feeling strangely empty sometimes. And that emptiness seemed more acute standing here with Oscar in his kitchen, smashing a pomegranate.

"Hey," he said, gently, the one who could always read her, the one who there was no hiding any of her secrets from, "we're supposed to be having fun."

It was too intense. She saw him too clearly.

He saw her too clearly. The six years separating them made it uncomfortable in ways it had not been before. Before they had been kids. Now they weren't. It added a sharply unexpected dimension to their relationship.

Molly did what she always did when she felt exposed. She pulled out her devil-may-care reckless persona.

"Oh, yeah?" she said. She took her dripping pomegranate-juice-stained hand, and made a swipe for his face.

He ducked out of the way. "Um," he said, reluctant laughter tickling across the beautiful firm line of his mouth, "maybe *I* should define *fun*."

"You? Define *fun*?" She scooped up some of the mash and reddened her hands even further. "No, I think I'll define *fun*."

He read her intent and dashed away from her. He put the sofa between him and her. "Molly, squishing pomegranate into someone's face isn't fun."

"I think it might be. I won't know until I try it."

Molly leaped over the back of the sofa. Oscar had expected her to try to come around it, but Molly was not one to do the expected.

He had seen the truth on her face for that split second.

She wanted to have children. She didn't trust herself to have children.

This was what was behind that "secret"— that she liked photographing babies.

And this was her way of trying to keep him from her truth. He vowed he would get back to it later. That's what friends did. They helped each other with truth. She had seen his instantly, hadn't she? That the death of his brother had exposed the weaknesses in his relationship with Cynthia.

And so, they would help each other outrun that truth until the time was right to tackle it. Oscar sprinted away from the threat of her little red-stained hands.

He felt laughter rise in him. He realized it had been a long time since he'd had a day like today: laughter, right in the bottom of his belly, rising to the surface, like bubbles rising in champagne, rolling out of him, chasing everything else away.

He circled, just out of her reach, back to the counter and doused his own hands in the massacred pomegranate.

"I'm armed," he warned her.

"Good. I couldn't have a fair fight with an unarmed man."

"You'll ruin your shirt completely."

"It's already ruined."

"No, I think we could save—"

She lunged at him. He shouted with laughter. They chased each other around the kitchen island and in and out of the living room furniture. He knocked over a lamp, and the vibration on the floor knocked one of the pictures on the wall crooked. The cat jumped off his favored chair, yowled once, protesting, then hightailed it down the hall. Oscar and Molly chased each other until they were both breathless with the sheer merriment of being silly.

"Stop," he finally said, pulling a dining chair in her path to try to slow her down. "I'm going to get a noise complaint letter from the condo association."

"Aw, that's a shame." She pushed past the chair. It toppled over with a crash. "You'll lose your gold star."

"No, seriously," he said, turning so he could face her.

"So long, Resident of the Month Award," she said, undeterred, charging toward him with her red mash hands.

He moved swiftly backward. "The neighbors are going to complain. This is not the kind of place where people stampede about like a herd of elephants."

He felt the hassock hit the back of his knees. He fell backward over it.

Chortling wildly, she was on top of him, squishing pomegranate into his face, until he could feel the juice running toward his ears. He retaliated, wiping his hand from her jaw to her cheekbone, and across her nose. It left a wide welt of red.

She snickered, then threw back her head and let loose a warrior howl that matched her face paint.

He shouted with laughter, condo association be damned.

And then he became very aware that she was on top of him. Her every curve was molded to him, the heavy chef's apron providing scant protection of his sudden, disconcerting awareness of her. Her scent—wild huckleberries on a sun-drenched day—filled his senses. The light from the kitchen shone behind her, illuminating her curls, each strand spun in gold. Her freckles were scattered across her nose like a mad toss of fairy dust had landed on her.

Oscar's laughter died abruptly. So did Molly's.

The air between them became charged with an electrical current.

CHAPTER SEVEN

MOLLY TOUCHED OSCAR'S FACE, not playfully now, but ever so gently, exploring. Then, she trailed her red finger, a pomegranate aril clinging to it, over his lip. His tongue, of its own volition, darted out of his mouth and took that seed from her finger.

The charge between them intensified, hissing and snapping like a storm-broken electrical wire on the ground.

The current held Molly and Oscar prisoner in its field. Oscar found himself helpless to resist the force that pulled him closer to her. He reached up, slowly, deliberately, and put his juice-drenched hand to her lips.

Everything intensified. The color of her eyes. The sensations along his skin. The sounds of both of them breathing. The delicate heave of her chest.

Molly's tongue flicked out, pink, soft, moist. She tasted the juice that clung to his skin, a hummingbird tasting nectar. He watched her eyes darken to a shade of green he had seen only once before, in a mossy and shaded dark corner of a forest.

And maybe once before that, even. After her father had died, and their lips had found each other in a moment so exquisite and so tortured it had burned a permanent etching in his brain.

He should have learned a lesson from that. He had felt things he had never felt before. But Molly had disappeared from his life as quickly as mist burned off by a hot sun, leaving him with a sense that the kiss had ruined everything.

Taken the most important thing in his life from him.

And yet, here it was again, the most delicate form of torture he had ever endured. Her lips, as soft as velvet, as plump as a ripe strawberry, on his hand, a gentle nuzzle that sizzled. Her eyes, wide and smoky, on his face.

He held his breath. Was she going to taste the pomegranate juice on his face, as well as his hand, with those delicate, exquisite lips? She leaned in toward him. He leaned toward her, pulled on a cord of desire that had been there for a long time between them. Invisible. But no less powerful for that.

Could it be different this time?

Was he willing to take that risk?

Did he have any choice?

The fire alarm shrieked at the same time he realized the burning smell was not his own heart going up in smoke.

They snapped apart from each other. She leaped up. He leaped up. The cat raced by them and hid under the sofa.

Despite the possibility the place was burning to the ground around them, they stood frozen, staring at each other. She should have looked hilarious, with her curls gone crazy around her clown-stained face. She looked anything but.

He whirled away from her. He had totally forgotten about sticking those bread rolls in the oven.

He must be forgetful these days. Because he had also totally forgotten the consequences of their last kiss. But he'd been lucky, this time. Fate had intervened before he ruined everything again.

He should have been more grateful than he was at the dark smoke that curled out of the oven door and hung wispily around the ceiling.

While he dashed to the oven and took the charred remains of the bread out, she grabbed a tea towel and stood under the smoke detector, fanning wildly at it until, with a final indignant whimper, it gave up.

"Eviction," he told her solemnly, "is imminent."

"But where will we live?" she asked, just as solemnly.

We. It seemed, for one insane moment, it wouldn't matter where he lived if she were with him. Molly could turn a cardboard box under a bridge into a grand adventure.

He turned deliberately from her and pulled the remains of the other item from the stove. She came and stood beside him.

"What was that?"

"A soufflé," he said. "Cheese. My first attempt."

"Maybe we could salvage it."

The soufflé took that moment to collapse completely in on itself.

"It reminds me of a building imploding," she offered, and then after a moment's consideration, "we could still eat it."

"It'll taste like smoke."

"We could pretend we're camping."

All of it an adventure, with her. Even the things that didn't go right. Maybe especially the things that didn't go right.

"It's pretty much my fault," she said. "It was the wrong time to start a pomegranate war. I can see that now."

She tried to look contrite, but her red-stained

face made it very hard to take her seriously. His face probably looked just about the same.

"There's a right time to start a pomegranate war?" he asked her.

"Oh, sure," she said. "There's a little spec of—"

She reached out to his lip. He caught her hand. They had literally been saved by the bell—or the alarm, as the case may be—and she could undo that with a single touch.

Wordlessly, he looked down at her. He wanted to lick every drop of that pomegranate juice off her face. He wanted her laughter-filled eyes to darken to that mossy shade of green again.

But he resisted all temptation, except one. He picked her up, his arms under her shoulders and her thighs, cradling her slight form against him. Her curls tickled his chin.

She didn't resist, either, but wrapped her arms around his neck. She sighed against him, and her breath whispered hot across his chest.

He had the unfortunate sensation of being a warrior with his plundered bride. Molly seemed to have surrendered to whatever might happen next. He could not allow himself to even contemplate the options.

There was only one option. They both needed some cooling off. He strode across the living room and slid open the sliding glass door to the deck with his foot. He took three long steps through the driving rain and across the smooth surface of the Italian-marble-tiled patio and leaped into the pool with her in his arms.

The water closed around them, cool and delicious. Just yesterday, he had not been the guy who would be leaping, fully clothed, into his pool, with a woman in his arms.

"You know what I like about you?" he asked, when they had both surfaced and were shaking drops of red-stained water from themselves.

"Everything?" she suggested, impertinent, despite the fact she was choking on laughter and water in about equal parts.

"Besides that."

"What?"

"Nothing ever goes as planned."

"Oh."

"Should we order pizza for dinner?"

"After we've had a swim," Molly said. "The water is glorious."

She tilted back her head and caught raindrops on her tongue. The tongue that had touched his hand.

"I can't swim in these clothes, though."

"I have suits—"

"Don't be silly, Truck."

A little late *now* for her to be telling him not to be silly.

"You've already seen my undies today. Plus, we've been swimming together in our underwear since we were kids."

She slid out of the apron and tossed it. Next came her wet blouse. She inspected the sleeve mournfully, then tossed the blouse on the deck and shucked off her trousers. They joined the blouse in a sodden heap on the deck.

This was not quite the same as glimpsing her panties through torn pants this morning. It was very evident to him, seeing her in her underwear now, that they were not kids anymore.

"Take off your pants," she invited him.

Nothing ever goes as planned, Oscar thought dryly. Not that he had ever planned her extending that particular invitation to him, but if she had, he would have hoped the circumstances might be different.

"Are you being shy?" she laughed. "I've seen your tighty-whities lots of times."

It was true. They'd always done this. Raised by her father, she'd never had the long list of dos and don'ts that most of the girls—and then women—in his acquaintance had had. There was nothing suggestive about her leaving her clothes behind if they became inconvenient. Molly had always prided herself on being one of the guys. She had never thought a single thing of stripping down to her underwear when their adventures had led them to the discovery of an unexpected swimming hole.

Not only would she strip down, Oscar remembered fondly, but she'd be the first one in the water, even in the spring, when you practically had to break the ice off of it to get in. And the tire swing hanging from a tree branch was never enough for her. No, she had to climb up the tree, to the top branch, as high as she could go, and swan dive into the water below. It was nerve-racking to watch her, even when you knew her stuntman father had been teaching her his crazy art at the same time she was learning to walk.

It occurred to Oscar that if he had thought he was lessening the danger between them by plunging them into the waters of his pool, he had made a serious miscalculation.

Molly was wearing underwear as utilitarian as the khakis she'd arrived at the airport in. He had seen bathing suits far more revealing than her black sports bra and her high-waisted white panties.

And yet her sliding through the water, effortless, strong, near naked, felt like one of the sexiest things he'd ever seen. And really more than his battered defenses could take. This new complication made him able to resist the temptation to be drawn back into the carefree world they had once shared—and the temptation to show her he no longer wore tighty-whities—and he hauled himself out of the pool.

"Towels are over there in the cabana when you need one. I'll go see about that pizza."

He needed a friend more than a lover, he told himself sternly. And the loss of his brother should make him very wary about loving Molly beyond the way he already did.

A woman who embraced danger was a poor match for a man who had learned the hard lesson that loving someone did not protect you from the loss of them.

It only made that loss, when it came, so much worse.

Molly floated in Oscar's pool, on her back, the rain splashing down on her face. As always, Truck was the reasonable one. He sensed the danger building between them and he'd walked away.

She, on the other hand, truly her father's daughter, never walked away from danger. She was invigorated by it. Exhilarated.

And the danger between her and Oscar had been as real as any she had ever felt, and she had experienced—and invited—many dangers in the quest for the perfect photograph.

In the quest to feel exactly what she was feeling right now.

Alive.

After a while, the pure joy of being alive lost some of its luster. Molly moved to the hot tub. She looked into the condo, craning her neck, but it looked dark. She did not see Oscar.

She waited, hoping he would see that moment of danger between them had passed and come back out.

But he didn't.

Finally, relaxed and tired despite the fact it was daytime in Germany, she got out of the pool and wrapped herself in a towel. On the way across the deck, she noticed raised planter boxes that she had not seen the night before.

There were neat rows of herbs growing in dark soil. Each was neatly labeled, all capitals, in his precise printing. *Basil. Oregano. Rosemary Thyme. Mint. Parsley.* Beside the herbs, two cherry tomato plants grew vigorously.

He was that guy. The guy you could rely on. He always had been. The guy who could keep plants alive. Thank goodness he had pulled away tonight, before she had given in to that thing that could wreck what he represented to her: the only stability she'd ever known.

She padded back into the opulent apartment. It appeared to be empty, a night-light shining above the range. The space was deeply silent. She crossed the open space to that granite and stainless steel marvel that was his kitchen. It was obvious Truck had gone to bed. He had left pizza out for her on the island. It was still in the box it had come in. He had also managed to salvage some of the pomegranate and left her a small salad.

She opened the pizza box and saw he hadn't even eaten. She was starving. She wolfed down the salad, grabbed a slice of pizza, then went and stood in front of the picture of Ralphie to eat it.

She felt the ache of missing him. What a good brother Oscar had been to Ralphie. His enjoyment of his brother had been so genuine. If he was playing football, Ralphie was included in some way on the team. If they went to a movie, Ralphie came along. Oscar, seemingly without effort, had made Ralphie part of everything. And it was Ralphie's joy in that inclusion that had made so many of the times they had spent together shine.

Oscar. The rarest of men. Decent. Honorable. Selfless.

She had all those things to thank for the fact she was sitting here eating cold pizza alone. He, sensibly, had kept them both safe from the danger of that passionate current that had leaped up between them.

Oscar had concluded, just as she had moments ago, that to give in to that passion could destroy their most valuable asset.

Their friendship.

Given that he was saving them both, why did she feel faintly resentful? Restless? Irritable with him?

Jet lag was making her unreasonable, Molly decided. She ate the last of her pizza crust and checked her phone.

Thankfully, some things were going according to plan. She made her way to her bedroom, showered off the pool water, and then she put on her plaid pajama bottoms and her T-shirt. She fell into the luxury of a very expensive bed, the crisp sheets announcing their thread count by feeling like silk against her tired body.

She told herself she probably would not sleep.

But she was asleep almost instantly.

CHAPTER EIGHT

OSCAR WOKE UP EARLY. Outside his window, he could see the rain had lifted and it was going to be a perfect summer day in Vancouver.

His space was silent, but that did not change the fact he was very *aware* that Molly was in it with him. On the other side of this wall. Curled up in bed, in her boy pajamas, her curls probably all squished to her head from sleeping on them wet.

For his own self-preservation, he'd abandoned her last night, and now as he lay there, contemplating her close proximity on the other side of the wall, he also contemplated the possibility of continuing with a strategy of avoidance.

But *he'd* invited *her*.

They were best friends. He'd known her since kindergarten. He probably knew her as well as any other person in his world. It was a sorry way for a friend to behave, to want to give her a ticket to go home as soon as possible.

How could he have forgotten how Molly complicated everything? She would definitely complicate his deliberately simple world.

And those complications seemed to be intensifying since the last time he'd seen her.

That wasn't quite true. It was the last time he'd seen her that had complicated everything. He could still—six years later—conjure the taste of her mouth, the dazed look in her eyes, the hammering of his heart, the wanting...

So easily triggered again, last night.

"Suck it up, buddy," he muttered to himself. He reviewed today's agenda. Shopping.

Molly had always been the quintessential tomboy. It was actually one of the things he loved—he stopped himself and edited that to *liked*—about her. She was unpretentious. Real. Molly in jeans with a rip in the knee and a too-large shirt knotted at her waist was more gorgeous than any model or movie star he'd ever seen.

She hated shopping, so today should be a cinch. In and out in thirty minutes.

He got out of bed. Though he normally would have just thrown a robe over his nakedness to go out to the kitchen, it now felt imperative that he be fully clothed around Molly at all times. See? Already, two minutes into the day, a complication in his simple routine.

Because normally, he would wander out to the kitchen, have a coffee, maybe flip through the news on his phone before showering and dressing.

Geez, he told himself, it's not that big a deal to change a habit temporarily.

It was only when he went to the kitchen, passing the photo of Ralphie, that an awareness—other than of his disrupted routines and Molly in his space—hit him.

It was the first time in eight months, one week and four days that he had not woken up with his first thought being of Ralphie. It was the first time he had woken up without the odd feeling of being crushed by the empty space that his brother's death had left in him.

Yesterday was the first time he had laughed like that. Let go like that. And it suddenly felt like a few complications were a small price to pay to be out from under the burden of this grief, even briefly.

Friends, he said to himself, like a vow that could not be broken. *We're just friends and it is going to stay that way.*

And here she came, his friend, just as he'd imagined—in those plaid pajama bottoms that were too big for her, and a plain white T-shirt that was also three sizes too large. Her feet were bare and her toenails, peeking out from under the too-long legs of the pajamas, were a shade of neon pink that was startling. Her hair was flattened to her head in some places and springing wildly away from it in others. There was a little print from the sheet tattooed across her cheek.

"Morning," she said, and yawned and stretched, way up high. Despite the fact the T-shirt was too large, it slipped up to show him the taut line of her belly. "You went to bed early."

"Uh—"

"You didn't even say goodnight."

"I didn't?" he said, raising his eyebrows, as if he were surprised.

"I hope you're not becoming a dull boy, Truck."

He hoped not, too, but sadly he thought of how the small change to his morning routine had grated on him. It reeked of dull, didn't it?

If he had not made and taken the *just friends* vow, he could take it as a challenge. And unfortunately, he could easily think of a way to prove to her he was not dull, right now.

"Early to bed, early to rise," he said, evenly.

"What's your plan for us for the day?"

She was trusting him to be predictable. Dull. And suddenly everything he did have planned seemed exactly that, dull.

"I was thinking a bit of sightseeing." The Vancouver Aquarium and the VanDusen Botanical Garden had been on his agenda today. Maybe the gondolas at Grouse Mountain, depending how time went.

"That sounds wonderful," she said, as if it weren't dull at all. "Should we get the shopping out of the way first?"

Out of the way. Hard not to love—correction: *like*—that about her.

She sighed. "Between the loss of the pants yesterday and the stains on the shirt last night, I could use a few things." She hesitated. She looked almost shy. "I need a dress."

James, he remembered sourly.

"It's not like you to need a dress," he said carefully.

She scrunched up her nose. "I know. I hope you'll help me pick the right one."

That was just the reminder he needed—that while he struggled, Molly was managing to still be *just friends* with him. Was he really going to help her buy a dress to wear for another guy?

"What's the occasion?" he asked, careful in his tone.

"A party. I'll be hopeless at picking that out. You'll help?"

Just what every guy wanted: to help a woman

pick something to wear for another guy. Would it be evil to help her pick something ugly?

"What's the party for?" he asked, casually, as if it were about helping her with the right dress choice and not prying into her relationship with James.

"O-oh," she stammered. "It's…um…a birthday party."

She had always been a terrible liar. Still no mention of James, the one she had promised to wear a dress for.

"What kind of a birthday party?" he pressed.

"A birthday party is a birthday party!" She said this a bit aggressively, because he suspected she didn't have an answer ready.

"Is it a child's birthday party? Or an adult's birthday party?"

The deer-trapped-in-the-headlights look let him know there was no birthday party.

"Both!" she cried.

"Okay. How far away is it? Because currently, your choices might be limited by the color of your toenails."

She looked at her toenails, then tried to tuck them inside her pajama legs, as if the wild color revealed something of herself she didn't want revealed.

"It's soon," she said. "I could remove the color."

"It's cute, though."

She blushed. Who blushed over the color of their toenails?

Complicated, Oscar thought with a sigh. She could cavort around the swimming pool in her underwear without a trace of self-consciousness, but try to hide her feet as if they were revealing some big secret about her.

He thought about that for a second. Her toenails were bright pink. What would that say about a person?

Feminine.

And passionate.

Molly's two most guarded secrets.

A friend would let her know it was okay to let those secrets out, that really, being a girl didn't have to be a cause for alarm.

Even if there was another *friend* involved.

Molly hated shopping. Dreaded it, actually. And yet her emails this morning confirmed that her plan was coming together for the celebration of Ralphie, and she would need something to wear other than what she had brought. She'd promised James a dress, which, given her plan, was silly.

But really, the sillier—the more fun—the better.

Besides, walking down the busy down-

town Vancouver street with Oscar at her side, the familiar dread she felt around shopping didn't seem to be there. She felt incredibly light, connected to him, ready for whatever the day held.

She hadn't felt like this for a long time. The swim last night—or maybe chasing him through the apartment before that—had awakened her senses, and they remai awake.

Of course, having one of the worl handsome men making you a coff second morning in a row—coffee t would have been proud of—m something to do with that. A noticed the color of her toer

It was those things ar being with him.

Again, today, the ge ory had been banisł side her was loos was like a maga haircut and pe who got pai their desk health, ge

If he were be "summer cas He was wearing a lig

tucked, tan cotton pants, canvas loafers with no socks. Sunglasses hid his eyes from her and completed that film-star look.

And yet, despite the fact his appearance was so sophisticated now, there was a solidness, presence and inner strength about Oscar that was the same as it had always been. It seemed to quiet her chaos. She was so aware of how lucky she was to have this man for her friend.

Don't wreck it, she warned herself, again.

"Let's try this one," Oscar said, holding open a door to a shop. She looked up at the sign over the door.

"Seriously? Elite? I think they have the ɔoty salesladies."

"Who are you kidding? What would you ɯ about Elite? You've never bought any- but Everest Outdoor in your adult life."

"u've barely seen me in my adult life."

"t's true."

"ch means you're reading the label on ɛ," she teased him, "and it's creepy. ɛks are their office-to-cocktails line,

"-drying as their outdoor line!" he ɛmber those pants being soaked

he said. "It's a miracle! Hang ɦower rod, dry by morning."

"Imagine Everest Outdoor being able to cover all your shopping needs. And probably from a catalogue, too."

"I also shop at Crockett and Davey for Women now. Less expensive. More durable."

"How's their dress selection?" His mouth lifted at the corner. "Durable?"

"I bet they could deliver overnight," she said hesitating at the door.

"I don't think they'll have suitable party dresses." He slipped off his sunglasses and turned the full force of those suede brown eyes on her. "Besides, you can't show off those toenails in hiking boots."

She looked down at her feet. "They're not exactly hiking boots. They're comfortable!"

"And durable," he guessed dryly.

"Yes!" Why was she defending her footwear? And what kind of weakness was it that suddenly she *wanted* to show off her toenails?

"When's the last time you bought a dress?" She lifted a shoulder.

"High school graduation," he guessed. "I remember that dress."

"So do I. It wasn't like anything any of the other girls were wearing."

"It wasn't?" he said, genuinely baffled. "I don't remember that."

"Well, I do and not fondly. It was too long, even with ridiculous shoes. Didn't I rip it before the night was over?"

He laughed. "Pretty sure you did. It wasn't really made for climbing trees."

"But I wanted to get that shot, looking down through the branches at the graduating class."

"Is that really the last dress you bought?" he asked.

"No. But to be honest, I don't have good taste in *girl* clothes. I'm counting on you to steer me in the right direction!"

He rolled his eyes. "I'm probably the wrong person to trust with this. I don't mind the…" he looked at her, searched for a word "…the girl Indiana Jones look."

"Really?" Coming from him, it felt like one of the nicest compliments ever.

"Really," he said, reminding her of why they had been best friends for so long. "But if you're going to give up that look, this is probably the place to do it."

The snooty saleslady zeroed in on them and came across the store like a battleship plowing through rough waters. If her look at Molly's best slacks—okay, maybe they were sporting a rather obvious crease where they had hung over the towel bar—and her T-shirt was faintly disparaging, all Oscar got was the brilliant smile.

"How may I help?" Her name tag said Barbara Kay.

Molly waivered. Her eyes were adjusting to the change in light from coming inside. The shop looked very expensive, with mood lighting and antique furniture scattered artfully about. Her sense of adventure abandoned her. She wanted the safety of same old, same old. She wasn't going to shop for dresses with Truck. What momentary madness had made her agree to that?

"What have you got in travel clothes?" she asked.

"Travel clothes?"

"You know, wrinkle-free? You can crumple them in a ball, throw them in your suitcase and put them on right away when you unpack?"

"Like what you have on?" The old battleship looked horrified and made no attempt to hide it.

"No," Oscar said smoothly. "We're looking for a special occasion dress."

"I'd be happy to help. Formal? Informal? Cocktail? Business?"

"I'm getting a headache," Molly said.

"Gorgeous," Oscar said, easily. "The perfect summer dress. In a brilliant color. Fun. Flirty."

"I'm not going to be flirting with anyone," Molly warned him in a dark undertone.

Something crossed his face. Surprise? Relief? Was he hoping she wasn't going to be flirting with him, then?

CHAPTER NINE

NOTE TO SELF, Molly thought, a little glumly. Truck did not want her flirting with him. Why would that bother her? It was so darned *wise*. Didn't he ever get sick of being the wise one?

"I don't like those kind of dresses," she told him. "The flirty kind."

"How would you know?" he shot back. To the saleslady, he said, "Please show us what you have."

"Here are summer casuals," Barbara Kay said, leading the way. "Let me know if I can help you find any sizes. When you're ready, I'll be happy show you the fitting rooms." She beamed at Molly before backing away.

The dresses were not squished together on racks, but displayed as if they were art pieces. Still, there appeared to be way too many to choose from. Molly turned over a price tag. "My headache is getting worse," she said mournfully.

"Why don't you pick three, and I'll pick three?" Oscar said. "How hard can it be?"

Reluctantly, Molly played along and went over to the "small" section of the circular rack closest to her. She flicked through them and chose one. She held it up.

"Navy is always practical," she said.

"It doesn't exactly sing *party*."

She gave him a mutinous look, held onto it and made her second choice. "And this one is good. A nice length to it."

He stared at the selection she held out to him. "What exactly do you mean by a *nice* length?"

"I won't be showing my panties to strangers if the wind comes up?"

"It's an outdoor party, then?"

"Yes."

"What would you say that color is?" he asked, carefully, focusing on the dress and not her frown.

"Beige? Leaning toward rusty brown?"

"I was going to suggest cat puke. Remember when you found Georgie in that hay barn?"

"He was so skinny," she said, smiling despite herself. "And scared."

"It took you a week to lure him out of hiding with cat food. And then, once he started eating, he wouldn't stop. He ate and ate and ate and then…that color. All over my shoes."

"Okay, okay, I'm putting it back, even though it's a perfectly respectable color that would go with anything."

"Except a party. Ralphie loved it when you wore bright colors," Oscar reminded her.

Suddenly, she remembered what all this was for. Had he figured out the party wasn't a birthday party at all, but a celebration to remember Ralphie? Was that why he'd mentioned his brother?

She looked at him closely. She didn't think so, but it changed the texture of the shopping trip, and erased her reluctance. It suddenly didn't feel as if they were in a high-end store, where she didn't belong. It felt as if that other world, the one they had shared, swam around her and held her up.

"Okay, okay, for Ralphie." It was truer than he knew. She chose the brightest colored dress off the rack and held it up for his inspection.

"That's better," he said. He called for Barbara, who must have been hovering close by. "We're ready for the fitting room."

"I've only picked two dresses," Molly said.

"Three, if you include the cat puke one."

"But I put it back."

"Clearly that's enough. I'll pick the rest."

"You're being very bossy."

"Because it's evident this is a topic you know

nothing about. That's why you invited me, re-member? I know. It's the blind leading the blind, but I'm willing to give it a shot."

Molly would have liked to complain, but she snapped her mouth shut. It was hard to argue with that. And it was a weakness, but she was just a little bit curious what Truck would think looked good on her.

"Think of it like princess boot camp," he suggested mildly.

"I've always been a better pirate!"

"You've always been a great pirate," he agreed, the affection rough in his voice, "but it's good to experiment."

"This from the guy who once blew up his mother's basement *experimenting*."

He ignored her and made his way along the rack of dresses. How was it possible he looked so darn comfortable sorting through the racks? It did a funny thing to her heart, seeing that strong confident guy so intent on picking just the right thing for her.

Far more intent than she was herself!

"You are so lucky," Barbara said, acting like her new best friend, now that she had caught a whiff of a sale. "How many men want to shop with their girlfriends? How enjoyable for you!"

She opened her mouth to say she wasn't his

girlfriend, but Barbara tucked her in a fitting room and shut the door.

It was, after all, *literally* true. Molly was a girl and she was Oscar's friend. And the saleslady was right. Why not just enjoy this? A treat. A break from her ordinary life. An opportunity to explore a side of herself that she didn't let out very often. An opportunity to be cared about. Looked after. And then she would surprise him with her gift—a tribute to Ralphie—before she left.

"Especially a man like him," Barbara cooed, through the door. "On the ooh-la-la scale, I'd say he's a perfect ten."

Molly thought of Oscar, the perfect ten, going through the racks, that look of intense concentration on his face she knew so well from when he was conducting science experiments. He'd already admitted that's what this was to him, some kind of experiment.

And that's what she should treat it as, too. An experiment. A new kind of adventure. Fun. Allowing herself to be pampered a little bit. To indulge that inner girl that she'd always been a little bit curious about. And wary of.

If there was anyone she could trust with this experiment, it was him, who genuinely thought she looked great when she didn't dress up at all.

Princess boot camp.

Good grief. The very thought brought a giggle to her lips. And Molly Bentwell, pirate, did not giggle!

By the time Oscar arrived in the mirrored area outside the fitting rooms, Molly had on the navy dress. It was a narrow shirtdress style and she was looking at it, over her shoulder, in the full-length mirror. She noticed he seemed to have quite a few dresses draped over his arms.

"I don't want to be here all day," she warned him.

He hung his choices on a hook outside the door of the only fitting room that was obviously occupied.

"Why? You have better things to do?"

"Ah, you know, ships to plunder, booty to be captured."

Something in his expression shifted ever so slightly at the word *booty*. She suddenly remembered it had several meanings that had nothing to do with pirates.

"We've already decided you're good enough at being a pirate. This is princess camp."

"Just a sec, I'll flounce and look pretty." She did her best to flounce. She blinked her eyes at him.

Oscar made a face. "A bit of work to do there. That dress looks great on you, but it's not what

I would call a party dress. It failed the flouncing test."

She considered that a mark in its favor, even for a party dress. "I think it's flattering. It makes me look very slender."

"You are slender. You'd have to fill your pockets with potatoes to not look slender. It looks like a guy's shirt. Against all odds, you've found the Crockett and Davey line of dresses. In Elite. The only time a woman should be wearing a guy's shirt—"

He stopped, suddenly uncomfortable.

"No, do tell," she purred, enjoying his discomfort. But then she thought of that. Of what it would feel like to be wearing his shirt, and what circumstances that might happen in. She changed the subject. Rapidly.

"The color is nice."

"I thought we agreed something to go with your toenails."

Had they agreed to that? She thought that was a bit of an overstatement. Still, she liked the way he looked at her toes, and remembered he'd called them cute. "It's silly to match a dress to toenails."

"Let's be frivolous," he suggested.

"You couldn't be frivolous if your life depended on it."

"Your bra strap is showing."

She tried to wrench it under the dress.

"That won't work. It's too wide. It's the wrong thing for that dress. Probably for any dress."

Molly felt her face getting very hot. "I invited you to help me find a dress, not discuss my underwear."

"If you had spinach stuck to your front tooth, I'd tell you. That's what friends do."

"My bra is like spinach stuck to my front tooth?"

"Figuratively," he said, and then laughed that Oscar laugh that made her love him, even when he was being annoying. "Figuratively? Get it? We're talking about your figure—"

"Okay, I got it," she said, faking far more irritability than she felt. "It's not funny if you have to explain it."

"Okay, let me explain this—your bra strap is showing, because it's too wide for that neckline." He regarded her thoughtfully. "Is that, like, a running bra?"

"It's like a none-of-your-business bra."

Undeterred, he leaned in and squinted at her bra strap. For an electrifying moment, Molly thought he was going to touch it. But no, he stepped back.

"It looks like something a woman weight lifter would wear at the Olympics."

Despite her protest, despite the fact the new electrical element was there, Molly found herself *loving* this interchange, bickering back and forth with Oscar. What a remarkable thing it was to have a friend who could be so honest with you, and who you could be so honest with.

Well, maybe not totally honest. She didn't really want him to know that the mere thought of his hand brushing her shoulder caused an electrical current to pulse through her.

"Barbara, can you…" He looked around. "Oh, never mind. I'll find one myself."

"Find one what yourself?" she squeaked.

"A bra. For you."

"You are not going to get a bra for me!"

"I am."

"It's not manly."

"I'm secure enough in my masculinity to handle it."

That was true. Oscar seemed a man so certain of himself that nothing could rattle him.

"You don't even know my size." Molly realized this was a bit of a retreat from a flat-out no.

He did, too. He grinned wickedly at her. "I bet I can guess."

"I bet you can't."

"You're on. Winner buys lunch."

She scowled at him, though she felt like laughing at the thought of her absent-minded scientist, Truck, sorting through women's underwear.

"Okay, since it's an outdoor party and the wind might come up, grab me some pantaloons, too." She might as well make the surrender complete. Did that mean she thought someone was going to see them?

"Pirates wear pantaloons. Princesses wear…"

"Ha! You have no idea what princesses wear."

"We'll see," he said. "I'm a man up for a challenge."

Truck wasn't, Molly realized, a little breathlessly, that absent-minded scientist anymore. He was a man who looked like he might know his way around women's underthings, which was a new and rather frightening light to see him in.

Frightening and thrilling, the two things hard for her to separate, as always. She bet he was good at kissing. Really good at it. Not that awkward boy who had comforted her, with his lips, shortly after her father's funeral.

Even then, it had been a wonder. To taste him in that way. To add that dimension to all the other dimensions of their relationship. She could have fallen toward that, what she had tasted on his lips that night, and it would have been like falling through a night sky, studded with stars.

Her eyes found his lips.

"What are you thinking about?" he asked, quietly. "Because either you still have pomegranate stains on your face, or you're blushing."

"I'm thinking about bras," she told him. "A topic I am not accustomed to discussing with members of the opposite sex. But since we are having this unfortunate discussion, no underwires!"

From inside the change room came the clear *ping* of an incoming message on her phone.

"Could you turn that thing off?" he asked, annoyed.

It was hard to annoy Oscar, but it was also proving very hard to plan an event on short notice.

"I can't, sorry. I, uh…have something going on."

He raised his eyebrows at her. "Are you going to tell him you're shopping for pretty dresses and underthings with a man?"

"Tell who that?"

"Whoever's texting you."

"It's probably work-related."

"Uh-huh."

Molly squinted at him. Was Oscar jealous?

Of course, he wasn't. He was just annoyed at her lack of techy etiquette.

"I can clearly see you don't need an underwire."

She folded her arms over the part of herself he could clearly see. It was his turn to blush ever so slightly.

"And no lace."

"Come on. It's pretty. Every princess should—"

"No. It's scratchy. And no—"

He took a step toward her. He looked down at her in a way that increased that breathless sensation. "That's enough rules, Mollie-Ollie. Trust me."

When he used that old nickname, a familiar little smile tickled across his lips. Had that smile ever made her want to kiss him before? Had it ever made her think of falling through a night sky, studded with stars?

That's what was making this dangerous! It wasn't two kids catching lightning bugs in jars on a hot summer night.

It was two adults discussing something only intimate partners should be discussing.

CHAPTER TEN

"I'LL PROBABLY REGRET trusting you with my lingerie choices," Molly muttered in an attempt to hide the hard hammering of her heart from him.

"I bet you won't," Oscar said, his voice a bone-melting growl.

Molly went back into the fitting room. She looked in the full-length mirror. There was nothing wrong with this dress! It went fine with her coloring. It was a good practical dress. One that could take you to meet a new client, or out for a drink. It might be okay on a short flight, or to do a really tame photo shoot.

He was right, though. It wasn't any kind of a party dress. Suddenly, seeing it through his eyes, she saw it was boring, just like he'd said, and she couldn't wait to get it off. And once she had it off, she looked at her underwear with a newly critical eye, too.

She suddenly couldn't wait to cover that up.

She put on her second choice for a dress. It was horrible. She had picked it only for the bright colors, but it was a two-layered dress. It consisted of a straight white sheath in a flimsy fabric she thought might be chiffon. The sheath was circled with layers of polka-dot-patterned ruffles, the polka dots all different sizes and every color of the rainbow. It seemed a bit like a child's party dress. She was going to take it back off, but decided it would be way more fun to pretend she liked it for Oscar.

Molly came back out of the fitting room just as he was coming back, his hands—unselfconsciously—full of frilly things. Frilly things in light pinks and sweet lavenders, brilliant whites and jet-blacks. She should have mentioned she liked only two colors for underwear, white and black.

She could feel a blush rising in her cheeks, again.

Oscar saw her like that? Like a woman who could wear those kinds of things?

"Look at this dress," she gushed. "Isn't it great?"

He skidded to a halt in front of her. "I like it."

"What?" She looked at him closely. Was he pranking her prank? "This is possibly the worst dress I've ever seen."

"It matches the toenails."

She squinted down at her feet. "I don't think it does. I think it may have every color on the spectrum, except that one."

"It's got a lot of movement," he said, approvingly.

She put her hands over her head and did a little hula move, her hips swiveling, the dress swishing around her. "I think it might be moving because it's possessed. By the ugliness demon."

"If you don't like it, don't buy it. But I think it's fun and perfect for a party."

"Ralphie would have loved the colors," she said softly, surprised by how suddenly serious she felt.

She realized, too late, maybe she had touched a tender spot, the one he didn't want touched.

But Oscar cocked his head and looked at it a different way. He smiled. "You're right. He would have. On the other hand, I don't think anyone would have placed Ralphie—or me—in charge of wardrobe selection."

She swung around playfully, in a circle, and the dress floated and flicked in the air around her.

His smile deepened. "You know, I think maybe you were right. The dress is horrible, and yet you carry it with a certain panache that makes me like it."

She spun around again, and the dress swirled around her, its abundance of ruffles rising and falling like feathers on a bird.

"That definitely would have been Ralphie's choice," Oscar said. He went quiet for a moment and gave his head a bit of a shake.

"What?"

"You know, today I've mentioned him several times, and I just realized, I haven't felt as if I would fall to my knees with grief."

"Truck," she said softly, "remember those overalls he loved so much? They drove your mother to distraction. She couldn't wait for them to wear out."

"I seem to remember, as soon as they did fall apart, you bought him another pair."

"Part of why your mother hated me."

"My mother didn't hate you," he said.

Oh, Truck, you have no idea.

"It's true, she didn't get you. Or your dad. You both thumbed your noses at the very convention she had adhered to so religiously her whole life. It threatened her."

Molly had never thought of his mother in that light. Mrs. Clark was so cool and so contained. Threatened by her? Not as scornful of her as she had appeared, but threatened?

"I think, after Ralphie was born, her sense

that she could control the world was snatched from her. It made her redouble her efforts."

She heard both sympathy—and the faintest aggravation—in his voice.

"Your dad—and you—challenged her view of the world. I think she was afraid I would like your world better than hers."

Threatened that Molly would draw her son away from her world? It presented that long-ago conversation in a different light.

"Did you?" she whispered.

"Oh, yeah."

That simple statement changed everything. And so did the wisps of smoke and spiderwebs that he held in his hands. He thrust them at her. He was actually blushing, which was totally endearing. "One of these will fit. And then I win the bet."

"If they are all different sizes here, you're guessing. You didn't really win the bet," she said triumphantly as she turned away from him.

"Here, wait, let me move these." He took the armload of dresses he'd hung outside the fitting room door and put them inside. He brushed against her and her every nerve felt as if it stood on end.

Had Oscar felt it, too? That electrifying jolt? Because he stopped, looked at her, then quickly backed out of the tiny space and closed the door behind him.

She sorted through the underwear, more self-conscious because he had selected it. They were all so delicate, so beautiful, so feminine. Somehow the fact he had chosen them made it feel as if each piece were burning her hands.

She finally chose a bra, a confection of spiderwebs and butterfly wings, slipped off her old one and put on the new one. Then she found the matching pair of briefs.

When she turned and looked at herself in the mirror, it felt as if she had slipped off one skin and put on another. She could feel herself going very still as she looked at her reflection in the mirror.

She looked *sexy.* She felt sexy.

It was just the fabric, Molly told herself. She was unused to delicate silks up against her skin.

She quickly took the top outfit off the choices Oscar had hung for her. It was a pale pink blouse, nearly as wispy as the bra, in its construction. The dark ruby skirt seemed very structured—not an improvement over the navy shirtwaist—but in fact, it was made of a stretch material that hugged her, and made her slender frame look delicately curvy.

"Pink is not my color," she called through the door.

"Tell your toes."

"Did you pick this just to match my toe-nails?"

"Yup."

She assessed the result in the mirror. It wasn't just an improvement; there was that sense, again, of having slipped out of her skin, of being brand new.

The skirt was really just a background piece for the blouse, which was gorgeous. It was sheer, gauzy, semitransparent. It felt as if she were wearing fog, and the silhouette of her new underwear peeked through, subtle, sensual.

"It's not really me," she called.

"Okay," he said. "Just pick the last one, and let's go."

"I didn't like the last one," she reminded him.

"I thought it grew on you? Show me this one. Let's compare. That would be the scientific thing to do."

Only he would think dress shopping could be turned into a science.

She didn't want to. She wanted to. Good grief! She was a woman who often placed herself in harm's way to get a photo—she couldn't possibly be scared to show Oscar this outfit, could she?

Taking a deep breath, Molly the princess stepped out of the fitting room.

Oscar gave Molly a grin, so slow, so loaded with frank male appreciation, that it felt physical, as if he had touched her, as if she were turning to butter, melting on a hot griddle.

"Nice toes," he said. He didn't even glance at her toes.

"It's not really me," she repeated.

"Isn't it?" he asked softly.

And in the way he said it, she saw a different her, the one she tried to keep as hidden as her pink toenails.

"You look beautiful," he said. "But then, you always look beautiful."

Beautiful. The fact that he found her beautiful—this man that she could trust for his absolute honesty—hummed along her skin.

"Could you find me some shoes that might go with it?" she asked, deliberately breaking the intensity of what was going on between them.

After that, it felt genuinely fun putting on her princess persona. For him. But mostly for herself. Molly embraced the role she was playing.

"What is it with men and stilettos?" she asked with fake chagrin as she waltzed out in the shoes he had found.

Oscar had exquisite taste—she had to give him that. The shoes added a subtle layer of sophistication to each outfit she tried on. And a not-so-subtle layer of pure—

"Sexy. They're sexy as hell," he growled.

She gulped at the spark in his eye when he said that.

Every dress he had chosen was different, and yet each seemed to celebrate her shape, each moved her closer to embracing her feminine side. Every time she modeled one for him, and saw the approval in his eyes, her confidence grew.

She was actually a little sad when she came to the last dress. She took it off its hanger, and even before she pulled it over her head, the fabric spoke to her fingertips. It had to be silk. It floated down around her. Except for the new underwear, Molly had never had a fabric touching her make her feel quite so exquisitely feminine.

"I'm not a yellow person," she called to him, turning slowly to stare at herself in the mirror.

"You said that yesterday. Remember von Goethe!"

"It has roses all over it. Like as big as cabbages."

"But they're pink," he called back, "remember our theme?"

"It's very loud. I don't like to call attention to myself."

"It's an experiment," he reminded her.

Her protests faded away. In all the other dresses, as beautiful and sexy as they had been, she had felt like a girl playing dress-up in her mother's clothes.

This dress made her feel as if, until this very moment, she had been a woman playing dress-up in a girl's clothes.

The dress was gorgeous, summery, fun. And yet, underneath all the summery fun of the color and the extra-big flowers, was an extraordinary fit that celebrated womanhood. It was sleeveless and, minus the thick strap of her regular underwear sticking out, it made her arms look lean and tanned and lovely.

The neckline was a deep V, much more plunging than anything she had ever worn. But, with the new underwear, it showed the snowy swell of her breast to sweet advantage. The waist was belted and the skirt flowed out from it, wide, wispy and full of movement. It ended at mid-thigh—way too short—but the way it swished around her legs made it an utter temptation.

One she had to resist!

"I'm going to take it off," she called through the door. She felt ridiculously shy, as if she didn't know who this person looking back at her through the mirror was.

"Okay. I'm getting hungry, anyway. You owe me lunch."

Suddenly, even though it felt as if it would take all the courage she had, Molly wanted to see this stranger who stood before her in the mirror through Oscar's eyes. She stepped out of the change room.

Oscar was silent. She watched his Adam's apple slide up and down the column of his throat as he swallowed. Then, he let out a low appreciative whistle. There was no smile this time. He met her eyes. "Now why wouldn't you want to call attention to yourself?" he chided her.

She lifted a shoulder.

"Don't tell me," he said softly, "that I didn't win this bet."

Had he won? Oscar asked himself. It was obvious everything he had chosen fit her perfectly, as if in his mind's eye, at some level of pure male instinct, he *knew*. He knew every sweet gentle curve of her.

But sharing this experience with her had created a deep and abiding awareness of the hunger in him that had nothing to do with friendship.

He had just made everything more complicated. But the look on her face—kind of a shy delight in herself—made it worth it.

Even as it called for him to be stronger than he had ever been before.

"Which one should I get?" she asked him.

"Get all of them."

"No."

"I'll buy them if you're worried about the cost. I want to get all of them, for you."

Most women would have loved that. Not Molly, of course.

"Uh-uh. I'm not the poor kid who hangs out with the rich kid anymore."

"I never thought of you as poor."

"Our house was practically falling down. My dad was employed sporadically. I never had the stuff the other kids had."

"You had such panache I don't think anyone—including me, really—ever thought of you as not having. You had things the rest of us didn't have. World travel experience. You met movie stars. And once you started taking photos, you seemed the furthest thing from poor. Rich in ways most people will never be."

This was Oscar: he could take the thing she felt the worst about, and somehow weave magic into it.

"You thought of me as poor," she challenged him. "You were always trying to buy me things."

"You never let me buy stuff for you," he reminded her sourly. "Stupidly, stubbornly proud. Sometimes at my expense. I *wanted* to see *Episode VII, The Force Awakens*, and you wouldn't go."

Speaking of the force awakening, he felt like a powerful force was awakening right now. In him. And in her.

"You could have gone with someone else."

"I did. I took Ralphie. But I wanted to see it with you." Then again, he would have probably been watching her changing facial expressions instead of the movie. He would have lived it vicariously through her reactions to each of the scenes.

That was how dangerous she was, he reminded himself. She could distract the world's biggest nerd from a science fiction classic.

She could distract him—a guy who considered himself very goal-oriented—from his goal.

A force awakening wasn't necessarily a good thing.

"When you're poor," she told him, "that's all you have. Your pride. Your sense of honor. You cling to it like you've found a log to ride down a swollen stream. I couldn't let you buy things for me."

"As would any guy who was completely besotted with a girl?"

Molly went very still. She looked at him with wide eyes. He realized he had said something that was as secret to him as her pink toenails were to her.

"You weren't!"

"Yeah, I kind of was. I mean not when we were five, obviously, and probably not even when we were twelve. It was when you came back from Africa that you seemed like this exotic, mature stranger. You had a style and a strength about you that took my breath away."

But, he reminded himself, when he had acted on that, she had rejected him. She had practically moved to a different planet. This wasn't how he'd pictured addressing this—in the middle of a women's clothing store—but he realized he had always wanted to address it.

"Then your dad died, and I kissed you. And my timing was the worst ever. I never got a chance to apologize for it. You were just gone."

He didn't know how far to take this. The truth was, he had not known how he was going to survive his world without her. She had been the fresh air blowing into a stuffy room. She had been the sunshine on gray days. His world without her had turned so bleak.

He felt wide open, and he didn't like it one bit. There was some unknown named James lurking in the background.

"Hey," he said, his tone forced in his own ears, coming across as flippant, "why don't I buy you the dresses to make up for it?"

"There is nothing to make up for," she said. "Nothing. I didn't go because you kissed me, Truck. I went because you were inviting me into a world I couldn't belong in. Not ever."

"That's not true." Somehow, this conversation had gone seriously off the rails. Things tended to not go as planned with Molly. Why hadn't he remembered that?

A lighthearted excursion to buy her a party dress turned into this: him making a mess of apologizing to her for something she had probably nearly forgotten.

"It is true. I can't fit into your world, Truck. Even the offer to buy the dresses shows that. Every one of these dresses requires a different set of shoes. It gets complicated. And I'd never get it all in my bag."

What kind of woman thought about being practical when it came to buying dresses? Though he was aware she was giving him a deeper message. And it was very true: around Molly, it got complicated.

"You could buy a new suitcase."

"See? It just becomes more and more stuff. I don't need all this stuff. I travel light, Truck."

Ah, yes, there was the hidden message in all of her photos, the one that he thought he might be the only one that could see it. The reminder of what kind of woman Molly Bentwell was. She traveled alone. And she traveled light.

That's why she had left after he kissed her. It required more of her than she could give. Or maybe more of her than she wanted to.

CHAPTER ELEVEN

"Rejected again," Oscar said casually, as if there was no sting at all to Molly's words that she traveled alone and traveled light.

"Don't say that."

He lifted a shoulder.

"You may buy me one outfit," she said, a little desperately, as if that could heal what she had hurt in him. That was one of the problems between them. It didn't matter what words you said. There was a deeper meaning.

"One," Molly said, holding up one finger, as if he might miss the point if she didn't. "But I'm buying the shoes. Which dress?"

It was obvious to him which dress. The yellow with the roses had been spectacular on her. "You choose," he said. "Surprise me."

She tilted her head at him and nodded. "Okay."

He tried to smile, but somehow he didn't feel like it. Somehow, it felt like whatever dress she chose was going to have a secret message.

Complicated.

Because then he remembered she wasn't buying the dress to surprise him. In fact, as he stood at the cash register paying for a dress that she wouldn't show him, it occurred to him he had just bought her a dress to go to a party with James!

As the transaction completed, her phone rang. She fished it out of her pocket and glanced at it.

"Oh," she said, "I've got to take this."

Speak of the devil, he thought, as he watched her walk away, needing privacy, apparently, a little smile on her face that made Oscar achingly aware how little he now knew about her new world.

Whoever that was, she'd been pleased.

"And just for your information," she said, when she came back, "I didn't really lose the bet because the sizes of stuff you brought for me to try on were all over the map."

Was she beaming like that because she hadn't really lost the bet? He wanted to ask her who had been on the phone, but it seemed way too "teenage boy."

"But the right size was in there." Oscar made himself follow her conversational lead.

She tilted her head at him and tapped her lips

thoughtfully with her finger. He really wished she wouldn't do that.

"I guess we could call it a partial win for you," she decided.

"What's that mean?" he asked, his grumpiness not all pretend. "Partial lunch?"

"Lunch, but nothing fancy. Do you have a favorite food truck?"

Somehow, he had the feeling she would think he was a complete dud if he admitted he had never eaten at a food truck.

"Not really," he said.

"After lunch, let's *do* something."

It seemed to Oscar they had been doing something, almost nonstop since her arrival. He suspected she wanted to put awkward conversations behind them. Who could blame her?

"I'm picking this afternoon's activity," Molly announced.

"And what can I look forward to?"

"A zip line, I hope."

That should, indeed, be a conversation killer. "Molly, have mercy, you know I'm afraid of heights."

She chortled happily. "We'll call it pirate school."

With her parcels wrapped up like she were carrying state secrets, they walked to a place where several food trucks congregated each day. Molly ordered the Zombie Special from Hong Bong. It claimed to be a fusion of Asian and West Coast culinary influences.

He ordered a plain burger from a nice plain-looking truck called Mike's.

They found a little park, and even though there was a very respectable-looking bench there, vacant, Molly threw herself down on the grass, belly first, legs crossed up behind her, propped up on her elbows.

He could see why Molly and dresses weren't necessarily a good match.

He eased himself down on the grass, gingerly, keeping a sharp eye out for any sign a dog might have enjoyed the spot before them.

"Want a bite?" she asked him, opening her food box and eyeing the contents with a certain rapturous delight.

The temptation to take food off the same fork she had used was countered by the appearance of the food: a mishmash of mushrooms, sprouts and unidentifiable items. He shook his head and unwrapped his burger.

"Delicious," she proclaimed. "How's yours?"

The aroma of hers was drifting up to him. It smelled delectable. His burger was predictable.

Which was what he liked…normally.

"You're not eating very much," she said,

looking at her own overflowing plate a bit guiltily.

Less to chuck up if the zip-line experience went as badly as he suspected it was going to. Not that he was going to admit that to her.

Which brought him to her plan for the afternoon's activities.

"About zip-lining," he said.

"Yes, I'm on it." Eating with one hand, she thumbed through her phone with the other. "Here's one. A two-hour tour. Is this close to here?"

She turned her phone to him.

"Unfortunately," he muttered.

"Oh," she read enthusiastically, "Zip lines reach speeds of eighty kilometers an hour and can be up to two hundred feet above the ground."

"Molly, you know I hate heights."

"Yes, I know. But I did something I don't really care for this morning."

"But it was your idea. Plus, I'm *actually* afraid of heights. You can see the difference between dislike and fear."

"You live on the fortieth floor of an apartment building!"

"You haven't noticed how I avoid the railing around the deck?"

She got that stubborn look on her face. He

loved that stubborn look, though it almost always foreshadowed trouble. For him.

"I did something I didn't like, and I enjoyed it," Molly said.

"You did?"

"Very much," she said. "So can't you try something you think you don't like? Please?"

Oscar had never been able to resist her saying *please* like that. He guessed they were going zip-lining. He finished his burger and stretched out on the grass.

Despite the looming threat of an afternoon suspended on a flimsy wire two hundred feet above the ground, despite some mystery guy named James, Oscar was aware of feeling happy.

That she had enjoyed shopping. That they were together. That the discussion of the kiss seemed to be behind them.

She put her phone away—apparently, her choice for a suitable zip-lining experience was made—and finished every bite of her food. Then she stretched out beside him. Her shoulder was touching his, and her hair was tickling the side of his neck.

Some women didn't need to wear a gorgeous dress to make a man so intensely aware of her that it felt as if his skin were tingling.

They stared up at the clouds drifting across

a perfect sky. She tilted her head and looked at him. The grass was making her eyes look greener, and her lips seemed puffy.

"Penny for the thought," she said.

Who is James? "We don't have pennies in Canada anymore."

Molly gave him a smack on the arm. "A nickel, then. Sheesh. Inflation."

He couldn't very well tell her that he was feeling stupidly jealous. And that even though the discussion of the kiss had gone quite badly, it seemed as if he had not learned one thing from it. Because he wanted to kiss her. To see if it could go differently this time.

And he wasn't admitting that to her. Not even for a measly nickel. Probably not for a million dollars.

"I feel really alive," Oscar hedged. It was not quite a lie. It was just not the full truth. "As if I can feel every blade of grass digging into my back, the sun on my face, the birds chattering. There's a hum, like the energy is rising from the earth."

"That doesn't sound very scientific," Molly teased him.

"I think it's probably a well-documented phenomenon, how everybody feels before they die."

She snorted. "You aren't going to die zip-lining. Besides, I haven't managed to kill you, yet. Truck?"

"Yeah?"

"Don't let me go to sleep. It'll wreck my whole jet-lag-avoidance program."

"I don't know. Sleep sounds like a great strategy for my whole zip-line-avoidance program."

She laughed.

He loved that sound. His feeling of drowsy happiness intensified. So long since he had felt this way.

Since Ralphie had died.

No, a voice inside him said. *Way before that.*

Since he had woken up one morning and Molly was no longer a part of his world.

Her phone started ringing, *again*. It was an annoying sound like the buzzing of a bee. She pulled it out, a little too eagerly.

"Hello?"

No doubt about it. She sounded breathless with excitement. He opened his eyes to squint at her—he hoped she registered the disapproval—but she just lifted her shoulder apologetically, and then walked away.

So she could speak in private. *Again.*

Thank God he hadn't confessed her lips were a temptation to him.

When she came back, she looked happy.

"Sorry, I have to cancel zip-lining this afternoon. Something has come up that I have to look after. Can I meet you back at your place in a couple of hours?"

Oscar digested that. She was abandoning him. She had been in the city less than forty-eight hours. She was going to go off on her own? Or was she meeting James?

"Can you take my dress home for me?"

Why did that feel like a relief? That whatever she was planning, she didn't need the dress. Still, she was in a strange place. She didn't know her way around Vancouver.

But Molly had been in strange places all over the world. She'd been in way more strange places than he had.

"What's up?" he asked, trying to keep his voice casual, the very same tone he would use if one of his guy friends announced a change in plan.

"It's something to do with work," she said.

She wouldn't meet his eyes. She was *lying* to him. The same as she had about the party she needed the dress for.

She'd always been the most horrible of liars. Why would she lie?

He was aware he felt worried. And protective.

But Molly wasn't the eighteen-year-old girl she had been when she walked out of his life.

She was an adult woman and feeling as if he *knew* her so deeply could be the greatest of illusions.

What if her ex had realized what he was losing, and had followed her around the world, and was begging her to come back?

Oscar tried to decipher the look on her face when she'd seen who was calling. Definitely pleased.

Another feeling overrode both the sense of being worried about her and the sense of wanting to protect her.

Anger. He was angry that Molly was here to see him and she was now dumping him to spend time with someone else.

He thought that over.

How could he possibly be mad that he *wasn't* going zip-lining?

Logically, he knew that after the way he felt about choosing underwear for her, and watching her come into some dangerous new part of herself in those dresses, that anger was the best possible thing he could be feeling right now.

A protection, like armor.

But for once in his life, Oscar found absolutely no comfort in logic.

CHAPTER TWELVE

HOURS LATER, WHEN Molly let herself back into the apartment, it was quiet. Really quiet, as if Oscar weren't there. But when she went down the hallway to her room, she saw his bedroom door was closed. It was silent but a light shone out from underneath it.

She paused outside it. Should she knock and tell him she was back?

She had a feeling he knew she was back and she was nervous about disturbing him. That was brand new.

Being nervous around Truck.

But she was hugging a little nugget of information to herself: he'd said he was besotted with her.

Mind you, that was a long time ago.

And all the same obstacles were in place, weren't they? Still, that admission made her feel edgy, and excited and frightened.

Because she had also been besotted with him.

What did all this mean right now? It was all so new it made her nervous.

But his anger was also brand new. It had been very clear when she had left him in the park this afternoon that he had been angry.

Once she revealed to him the reason she had abandoned him today, it would make everything okay. She knew it would. For all the exciting things she had done in her life, this felt the most thrilling.

Doing something for him. Something great for him.

But, meanwhile, she had to digest this new thing: Truck, on the heels of admitting he'd once been besotted with her, was angry.

With her.

Of course, she had seen him angry with other people. Not often. He was a man extraordinarily slow to anger. But when Molly had seen him angry, it was usually around Ralphie. He had never been able to tolerate any kind of meanness toward Ralphie. Even curiosity, people staring at his brother, sometimes made him angry.

"I can understand little kids staring at him," he'd told her once. "But their parents? I'd like to go over there and knock their heads together."

That anger transformed him. It showed an innate power in him that he did not unveil very often. But when he did, he became a warrior, that man who was willing to lay down his life in the protection of those he cared about.

But this was a strange thing to have him angry with her. She had hoped to come back, and maybe try cooking together again. A swim in the pool. Maybe they could discuss the besottedness a little more. Maybe, she could expand on not fitting into his world, and why she felt that way…

Instead, there was note saying the pizza was in the fridge for her.

Cold pizza. Alone. Again.

It was so much smarter than what had transpired between them last night. And yet, she felt robbed. Sad in a way she had rarely felt sad, that Truck was a breath away from her, and apparently they were not speaking.

There was also the secret to consider. If she spent time with him tonight, would she be able to keep all this bubbling excitement to herself, or would she spill the beans?

So cold pizza and an early night it was.

When Molly got up in the morning, she had a text from Oscar saying he'd gone to the office.

She felt a moment's panic. Was he going to wreck everything? She sent him a text back.

I thought we were going to hang out together.

There was a long pause before he answered.

That's what I thought, too.

Can you set aside the afternoon for me? It's important.

Not if it involves zip-lining.

It doesn't. I promise.

What does it involve?

It's a secret.

It seemed like a long time dragged by before he answered.

Okay, I'll be back by noon.

Molly set down her phone, nearly trembling with relief. Her eyes flew to the clock. Noon! So much still to do.

Oscar, always punctual, came through the door at a few minutes before noon. He stopped and stared at her.

"That's the dress you chose?" he asked. He looked like he didn't want to smile at her, but he did anyway.

Molly did a pirouette for him. The polka-dot ruffles swished around her.

"You know only you could wear a dress like that, with those boots, and somehow look as if you are setting a trend, not posing as a hillbilly, circa 1935."

"You know me," she said. "An on-trend kinda girl."

"I'm not sure I do know you," he said, and she could tell a bit of that anger was still there.

"Come on, we have to go."

Shaking his head, he followed her out the door.

"We're going to this address," she said, showing him the address on her phone. She could feel the anticipation building.

"I don't recognize that address."

"Can you put it in your GPS?"

He complied and they wove away from downtown Vancouver and out into the suburbs. And then they left the suburbs behind.

Finally, they came to what appeared to be an empty lot behind a chain-link gate that hung open on its hinges.

"Look," he said, impatiently, "you better

start explaining. This is the kind of place shady deals go down."

"Trust me."

He looked insultingly uncertain about that. Then he squinted at the sign that hung crookedly from the fence. "Mad Mudder's? Where are we? And why?"

"You'll see," she said. She'd found her way here yesterday and despite the look of the place, it was going to be perfect.

They pulled up to a small shed. A man came out. Thankfully, he looked crisp and professional in a matching khaki shirt and pressed slacks.

"Molly," he said, "It's nice to see you again."

Oscar slid her a look out of the corner of his eye before taking the hand that was being extended to him.

"I'm Tracy Johnson."

Then he stepped back and regarded her with a frown. "Did you bring something else to wear? I told you yesterday, it's a pretty extreme experience."

"Yesterday," Oscar said, looking at her quizzically. "This is where you were yesterday? What exactly is this place?"

"You didn't tell him?" Tracy asked.

"It's a surprise," she said.

"Oh. Well, welcome to Mad Mudder's team-building experience."

Oscar shot her a look. "This is in some way preferable to zip-lining?" he grumbled.

"Where's everyone else?" Tracy asked.

"Everyone else?" Oscar asked, just as another vehicle came down the road and turned into the rutted driveway. It was a seven-passenger van. The windows were tinted.

Molly did not look at the van. She could not take her eyes off Oscar's face as the side door slid opened. He shot her a quizzical look. She realized she was trembling with excitement.

"I didn't do it right on Ralphie's birthday," she whispered. "I thought the actual day should be quieter. More reflective."

The van stopped. The door slid open. And one by one, they came out. The three remaining members of Ralphie's Special World Games relay swim team, and their coach, Mrs. Treadwell.

Oscar turned to her, understanding dawning in his face.

"What is this?" he whispered.

"Our celebration of life. For Ralphie."

His eyes rested on her face, and what she saw there stopped her heart.

"It's good to see James again," he said quietly. "I heard you mention his name on the phone, but I never put two and two together. It's so good to see them all. Fred. Kate. Mrs. Treadwell."

But it felt as if the one he was really seeing was her, Molly, and what was in his gaze was enough to stop her heart. Unless she was mistaken, Oscar was still as besotted with her as he had ever been.

Or perhaps she just saw the pure love in his face. Not just for her, but for all of them.

But maybe, just maybe, there was a special place in his heart for her. For having, somehow, someway, gotten this just right. The way a best friend should.

He smiled at her, and the warmth of that smile felt as if it could carry her through frozen days and winter nights and storms of all kinds.

And then he was engulfed in the team. From her phone calls to set this up, Molly had found out that, like her, Oscar had kept in touch with the members of his brother's old swim team. As per the rules, each participant was only allowed to compete twice in the Special World Games, so the team had not been together for a number of years.

The time gap only served to make the reunion more poignant for all of them, but Oscar was definitely the star of the show. His brother's teammates were surrounding him, touching him, hugging him, calling his name. Molly knew they loved her, and she would get her turn, but he was first for them, the man who had been the big brother to them all for the years that Ralphie had been part of the Special World Games team.

Truck had often said to her one of Ralphie's gifts to him was that how people interacted with Ralphie showed him who they really were.

This was also true of watching him with the old team. Watching him at the center of all that affection Molly could see, so clearly, who Oscar really was, and who he had always been.

Strong. Reliable. Decent.

It was a beautiful chaos. Hugs. Tears. Shouts. High fives and ruffled hair and secret handshakes. Oscar knew all the secret handshakes.

He was a man with such a good heart.

They turned from Oscar then and swarmed around her. She was engulfed in all that love, but it was Oscar's smile that was at the center of a heart that felt filled to overflowing. It was a smile that put the stars out at night and drew the sun from the darkness in the morning.

"Ralphie," Oscar said, turning to Molly, finally, his arms thrown over the shoulders of Ralphie's friends, Fred and James, his eyes just ever so faintly misted, "would have loved that dress. Thank you for choosing it for him."

Truck got it. He got it so completely, that it felt as if her heart were going to burst with happiness.

Finally, Tracy blew a whistle and held up his hand. "Okay, so you people have to divide up into two teams. And then you have to get through that obstacle course. You have to figure it out together. The first team through wins, and there is a very special prize for them. They get to throw the other team in the mud pit at the end."

This announcement was met with roars of approval.

"How do we pick teams?" Mrs. Treadwell asked.

"That's part of the exercise," Tracy told them. "You have two minutes."

"I want to be on Oscar's team," Fred shouted.

They were all jumping up and down with excitement. They all wanted to be on Truck's team.

Molly saw something she had never seen on Oscar's face before: panic. No matter how the teams were divided up, someone's feelings were going to get hurt. He was the sun that they all wanted to rotate around. Including her.

"One minute," Tracy called.

Mrs. Treadwell cleared her throat.

"I think it should be the four of us—me,

Fred, James and Kate against Miss Bentwell
and Mr. Clark. We haven't trained together for
some time, but we've already worked as a team.
Frankly, I think we'll kick some butt."

CHAPTER THIRTEEN

THERE WAS PANDEMONIUM after the butt-kicking pronouncement. Mrs. Treadwell's team solidified instantly, high-fiving, and calling happy jeers at their opponents.

But Molly felt something go very still in her. She and Truck as a team. Working together.

"Name your team," Tracy called. "Thirty seconds."

"Down Under," Mrs. Treadwell called.

"Truck Stop," Molly suggested.

Tracy provided coveralls: blue for Down Under and orange for Molly and Truck, but Molly refused hers.

"You'll ruin that dress," Truck told her, gamely putting on the coveralls.

"For a good cause!"

"You can't wait to wreck that dress," he guessed, laughing.

"You're so right. And you'd better hope the sheriff doesn't show up, because you look like

an escaped convict," she said. Then she flicked
up the edge of the skirt. She had shorts on underneath. He threw back his head and laughed
even harder, and right then she knew it was
going to be wonderful to be a team.

They were allowed to inspect the two iden-
tical courses that ran side by side.

There were smaller obstacles, but Oscar and
Molly quickly identified the four tough ones:
crossing a very narrow log; a rope swing over
water; a huge straight wall; and a crawl under
strands of barbed wire. There were all kinds of
rules about finishing obstacles together, as a
team, that increased the level of the challenge.

At the very end of the course, with a little
more glee than might have been strictly neces-
sary, Tracy showed them the mud pit that the
losers would be thrown in.

"Throwin' you in the mud," Fred called joy-
ously to Oscar.

"Throwin' you in the mud," Oscar called
back.

"Do you think we should let them win?" she
whispered.

"They would hate that. Besides, it's not in
your blood."

And then the starting whistle blew, and he
proved that was true. Oscar was fiercely competitive. Having grown up with a disabled

brother, he knew there would be no worse insult than "letting" the other team win.

She was fiercely competitive, too. Often, that competitiveness had come out between them, and so it was invigorating to switch channels and to work as a team.

And it was delightfully astonishing how quickly they became one mind, how they played seamlessly together.

It was glorious to see Oscar in this element, both his enormous physical strength and his brain power being put to good use. After some trial and error, they put the first two obstacles behind them.

But a new obstacle between them was not being conquered at all, instead it was growing in size and intensity and their inability to navigate it. The obstacle course had obviously been designed for teams of four.

With just the two of them, they quickly realized getting through most of these challenges as quickly and as efficiently as possible was going to require that they practically be glued together.

There was laughter. And heated discussion. Evaluation of the other team's progress.

And underneath all that, something else brewed and sizzled, growing white-hot. He piggybacked her across the log. They clung together on the rope swing. They fell off on their first attempt, and now, soaked, the physical awareness between them intensified.

Molly was drunk on the heat of his skin. The beat of his heart. The play of his muscles through the thin fabric of the dress.

She was drunk on the fact that once he had been besotted with her. And it seemed as if he might still be.

The electricity between them translated into energy. It looked as if Truck Stop was going to smash the opponents. But then they came to the wall.

It simply was not a two-person challenge.

Oscar somehow managed to scale to the top. He hung over it on his belly, reaching out his hands to her, but no matter how hard she ran, and no matter how high she jumped, she couldn't reach his outstretched hands.

He turned over and slid back down the wall. He crouched down.

"Get on my shoulders."

She scrambled on. She could feel the simple strength of him as he lifted her up. She stretched as high as she could. No dice.

"They're gaining on us," she cried. As she watched, dismayed, Down Under came to their own wall. They stood around it, chatting, and then quickly formed a human pyramid. And then they were over it and gone, out of sight, their shrieks at victory in sight in the air.

She stretched higher. She stood on one foot, trying to just get that little bit more height... She wobbled.

He tried to stabilize her but it was too late. She was falling off his shoulders.

And then she was in his arms.

Blinking at him. His strength closed around her. The obstacle course, and the yells of the opposing team, faded.

It felt as if it were just she and Oscar in all the world.

"Should we finish what we started all those years ago?" he growled.

"Yes," she whispered.

His lips were dropping over hers.

He was tasting her. She was tasting him. It was exquisite.

But just like last time, the timing was terrible. The place was all wrong. There couldn't be a less romantic setting in all the world.

And yet there was no denying what was unfolding inside of her.

She had waited her whole life for this exact moment.

To finish what she had started. With Oscar. With her Truck.

She was aware she had wandered aimlessly

in the desert since she had left him. Nothing had ever filled the hole that had been left. Not her successes. Not her relationships. Not her moves from one city to another.

She could see so clearly now that each of those things had just been an attempt to outrun the hole in her heart.

The hole that only he could fill.

She sighed into him. She surrendered into this moment, which felt as if she had waited her whole life for.

Homecoming.

And then it was over, as quickly as it had begun. Molly found herself unceremoniously set on her feet.

She opened her eyes and looked at him. He nodded over her shoulder, and she turned around.

The whole Down Under team was staring at them.

"Were you kissing?" Kate asked.

"Um, sort of," Oscar said.

Kate cocked her head at him. "How do you *sort of* kiss?" she asked, guilelessly.

Molly looked up at him. He was blushing.

"Uh, Molly was on my shoulders, trying to get over the wall and she fell. I was just, um, making sure she was all right."

"Like her lips were all right?" Katie asked dubiously.

"Like a get-better kiss," Fred told Kate officiously.

"Yes!" Oscar said, "Just like that. Have you guys finished the course?"

"No, we're waiting for you."

"You're going to win. We can't get over the wall," Oscar said. "It's not a challenge for two people."

"It wouldn't be fair to win like that," James said. "It would kind of be like cheating, because we have four."

Molly looked at Oscar. She could see the emotion in his face.

Because this was grace. A Ralphie moment if ever there was one: the generosity of it; the pureness of heart; the inability to put competition above decency. Love trumped all.

"Here," Fred said. "We'll help you."

And so the pyramid was reformed, and Oscar was put on the top of the wall to help haul people over.

None of them ran to the next obstacle, barbed wire. They ambled over to it, and helped each other get through it.

Even with help, Molly's flimsy dress got ripped to tatters. Everything underneath it did, too, the shorts not quite providing the protection and privacy she had hoped for!

She thought Oscar might try to remove himself from the intensity of what had just happened between them, but no.

In a voice only for her, filled with the sensuality of smoke and fog drifting in a forest, he growled, "I see you wore the pink."

She knew that stolen kiss was not the end of it. A beginning. It felt as if she were standing at the edge of a cliff.

With no rope and no parachute.

"Well," Tracy said, "I have to say I've never seen one unfold quite like that before. Who's the winner, and who goes in the pit?"

Fred looked at him with baffled innocence. "We're all the winners," he said, as if that was the most obvious thing in the world.

And then they raced to the edge of the mud pit, and one by one they took each other's hands, until all six of them stood there.

"On the count of three," Oscar said.

Screaming with laughter, holding tight to each other's hands, at the count of three they all yelled, "*Go for it*," and then they leaped.

Mid-air, Molly realized this simple truth: a hand to hold was the rope, and love was the parachute.

* * *

"Everybody's coming to my place," Oscar announced, after they had all hosed off. "Pool and hot tub. What do you guys want for dinner?"

"Pizza," they yelled in unison.

"Are you okay with pizza one more time?" he asked Molly.

"It's not a soufflé kind of crowd," she told him, laughing.

The Down Under team clambered back in the van, which would follow his car back to the city.

"I'm going to wreck your car," Molly said, getting in gingerly. "Truck! You'll never get it clean."

No, he probably wouldn't. And, given the mud on everyone, his apartment was probably never going to be pristine again, either.

None of it mattered.

"You did all of this?" he said, turning on the heater when she shivered. "For me?"

"For me, too."

"So, getting everybody here, booking plane tickets—"

"Hotels, the van, the venue. There were a few times I just wasn't sure if I could pull it off, but it turned out pretty good, huh?"

He contemplated that. *Pretty good?*

"Molly," he said softly, "I have never received a gift like that one. It was exactly right. Perfect from beginning to end."

Including, he thought, a bit uneasily, that kiss.

And her pink underwear.

And a sense of the future stretching ahead of them, unknown. It was like that broken electrical cord on the ground, again. Sparking.

Electricity, tamed, could be a good thing. It could provide light and warmth and comfort and convenience.

He glanced over at her. She had mud on her face. Her hair was plastered to her head. Her clothing was soaked and clinging to her. Her pink bra was peeking through what was left of that dress.

Awareness of her shivered through him. Right now, she looked more beautiful than she had looked in that yellow dress and the stilettos. In fact, Oscar was not sure he had ever seen a woman as gorgeous as Molly.

Electricity, untamed, could be a bad thing. A single spark could burn a whole forest down.

CHAPTER FOURTEEN

UNTIL MOLLY HAD arrived Oscar had never considered that his apartment was missing something. Cynthia had insisted on hiring a designer and each—expensive—decision had enhanced an already beautiful space. His home was perfectly decorated *and* functional, not just pillows and poof.

The kitchen—with its double ovens, built-in coffee maker, wine cooler, stand mixer—would have made a professional chef happy.

In the living room, a seventy-five-inch television hid behind a piece of canvas wall art that rolled out of sight at the push of a button.

The pool, and spa, the exquisite outdoor entertaining area furnished with all of his own creations, was outside the door. The views were jaw-dropping.

The space quietly proclaimed arrival. It had everything a man could ever dream he wanted.

But right now, Oscar's apartment had never

looked so bad. There were towels on the floor and draped over the leather sectional. Half-eaten slices of pizza seemed to be everywhere. White square boxes, grease-stained, with leftovers in them, were scattered about randomly.

A soda had overturned, and despite Molly's and Mrs. Treadwell's frantic efforts to sponge it up, there was a dark stain on a carpet that Oscar knew to be worth more money than his vehicle.

So, his apartment had never looked so bad. And it had never felt so good. He had called it home before, but it had not felt that way until now, filled to overflowing with Ralphie's friends. They were jumping in and out of the pool and hot tub, running around outside, coming into the apartment, dripping water on the floor. Oscar knew, with sudden clarity, exactly what ingredient had been missing from a space filled with spectacular things and stuff.

Life.

Molly had been right. Before it had been a movie set. Now, with Molly at its center, it teemed with life and his gaze kept seeking her out.

She had made a great ceremony of tossing out the dress when they got back to his apartment. Then, she had found the ugliest bathing suit in his guest collection—leaving the nicest one for

Katie—and led the charge to the pool. Now she was in her pajamas, two cameras around her neck, her feet bare, working unusual angles to get those great shots she was famous for. If that meant standing on the granite kitchen island, or crawling under the coffee table, or straddling the back of the sofa, that's what she did.

Finally, things seemed to be winding down. Bathing suits were fluttering from the balcony railing—strictly against condo rules—and Fred and James and Molly were sprawled out on the carpet on the floor. Kate and Mrs. Treadwell were on the sofa. Oscar was in his easy chair. Even Georgie, who made a point of hating people, could not stay away from the love in the room. He had crept in and found a place on James's lap.

Oscar did not know how much he had waited for this moment, until it happened.

"Remember how he loved Uranus?" Fred asked quietly.

The Uranus stories started. They all had one. They could all remember a time Ralphie had cornered some unsuspecting stranger and begun an earnest discussion of his favorite planet.

Of course, his love for all things Uranus had only deepened when he discovered people thought he was saying *your anus*.

By the time each of them had shared a story, they were all howling with laughter. The flood-gates had opened and they told stories about Ralphie deep into the night. Some of them made them laugh and some of them made them cry.

Mrs. Treadwell fell asleep on the couch. So did Katie. Molly brought out blankets and pillows. At one in the morning, Mrs. Treadwell woke up and declared the party over. Between the obstacle course, the pool party and stuffing themselves with pizza and soda, everyone was so exhausted they didn't even protest the party's end. The van was called to bring them back to their hotel.

At the door, there were tears and hugs and kisses and promises.

And then the door whispered shut, and something else happened that Oscar was not aware he had waited for, until it happened.

He and Molly were alone.

Molly went back into the living room and looked in one of the pizza boxes. She picked up a very dead looking piece of pizza, plumped up one of the pillows, sank down on the sofa, pulled a blanket over herself and took a bite.

"That's going to—"

"Anchovy," she declared with a blissful sigh

before he could finish his sentence. She was pretty sure, Oscar being Oscar, he planned to warn her the pizza was going to be cold, not to mention have a potential food poisoning hazard.

It was nice to have someone care about such things. "Should we watch a movie?"

"Aren't you exhausted?" Oscar asked her.

"Sorry, no. It's almost lunchtime in Frankfurt. Are you exhausted?"

"Yeah. No movies for me tonight."

"Go to bed, then."

So silly to be so happy that he didn't go to bed. Instead, he came over to the couch and said, "Scoot over. I'm too happy to go to sleep."

She pulled back the blanket, inviting him in, and he climbed in behind her. She leaned on him, munching her pizza. Maybe it was the pleasant exhaustion that enveloped him, but he touched her hair.

She didn't protest. In fact, she leaned deep into his fingers, like a cat who wanted to be stroked.

"Best day ever?" she asked him.

"Without a doubt."

"What happened between you and Cynthia?"

"Why end the best day ever with *that*?" he asked back.

"It just seems like the time of night and the

kind of day that encourages confidences," she informed him.

"That's true. The long day has lulled me into a state of languor that makes me want to tell you my whole life story, except you already know that."

"So, fill me in on the bits I've missed out on." She nestled deeper into the solidness of him behind her.

"Something was missing with Cynthia and me. I'm not even sure I knew what it was until tonight when I saw my apartment filled with laughter. And light. And love. Everything with Cynthia looked so good, but..." His voice trailed away.

"Just like your house that you grew up in. I see that in a different light since you mentioned when your mom's control issues started."

"I don't know that they started with Ralphie. But I think that made them worse."

"Everything was just so perfect. Like a stage set. Coming from my place—Dad's motorcycle parts on the kitchen counter—I loved it. And maybe even envied it, a bit. And was afraid of it, too. It had an unspoken look-but-don't-touch vibe. Looking back, it lacked...er...soul. Except for you. And Ralphie."

"I think I knew it couldn't work with Cynthia even before Ralphie died. We were planning the wedding—*she* was planning the wedding, I should say—and I was going along, because she was doing a fantastic job and didn't really need much input from me."

"But?"

"I had one request, which I considered nonnegotiable. I told her Ralphie was going to be my best man."

Molly twisted to look at him. "She said no?" she whispered.

"She didn't say no. It was just the look on her face. Something in me quit right then, though it wasn't until after he died that I realized how badly it had unsettled me, how much of a wedge it had put in the relationship. That look haunted me. I guess, I had always thought he would come live with us, one day. After Mom and Dad couldn't look after him anymore. But that look…"

"How could he *not* have been your best man?" Molly asked, chagrined.

"Well, no doubt he would have blurted out *Uranus* at exactly the wrong moment."

"But that would have been the best part," Molly said.

"Yeah," he agreed softly, "I think it would have been."

"How come he died? I've been scared to ask this—"

"Don't ever be scared to ask me anything."

"I just didn't want to hurt you if you didn't want to talk about it."

"I like talking to you about it," he said softly, as if that came as a surprise to him. "It makes me feel not quite so alone with the grief."

"Me, too," she said. "Eight months, one week and six days."

His arms tightened around her. Did his lips touch her hair?

"When you called to tell me," Molly said softly, "you said he just went to sleep one night and didn't wake up. He was only twenty."

"His heart stopped."

"All those years of swimming," she offered pensively, "and he never seemed to have a health problem."

"It went undetected, though lots of people with Down syndrome have heart problems. Fifty years ago, it was rare for someone to make it past twenty-five, now their life expectancy can be in their sixties. They think it's partly because they used to be unfairly institutionalized. They do better at home, surrounded by family."

"Of course, they do better at home. Sheesh!"

Someday, it would have been Oscar's home. Where Cynthia would not have welcomed Ralphie. She knew it wasn't fair to hate someone you had never met, but Molly didn't let that stop her hating Cynthia just then.

"Ralphie had such a good heart, spiritually, if not physically. I guess I took it for granted that he was always going to be part of my world," Oscar said softly.

"I'm so sorry, Oscar."

He smiled sadly. "I like to think his great big heart just outgrew his body."

They sat with that for a bit, quiet, comfortable with each other's sorrow.

"What happened between you and your latest?" His finger was wrapping one of her curls, unwrapping and then wrapping it again. She wished he would kiss her head again, so she could be certain that he had.

"I found panties under the bed. Not mine. Maybe that's why I'm sensitive to underwear discussions."

"You deserve so much better," he said quietly.

"You, too."

"I meant in the underwear department," he said.

And then they were both laughing again.

"Maybe you deserve better in that department, too," she said. "How would I know? I haven't seen them, yet."

Yet?

Thankfully, Oscar didn't pick up on her Freudian slip. In fact, Molly could feel the spaces between his breaths get longer, and his finger remained in her curls, but he wasn't playing with them anymore. The rise of his chest was steady and strong.

A man with a heart every bit as big as his brother's had been.

Feeling as safe, as secure as she had ever felt, Molly let her eyes close. Sleep enveloped her.

When she woke up, she had a sore neck. She glanced at her watch. She was turned around despite herself. She had only slept a few hours. It was 6:00 a.m.

Still, sleep deprivation aside, she had a good feeling. A delicious feeling. Oscar was still behind her, propped up on the couch cushions, his arms wrapped around her midriff, his breath stirring her neck. The scent coming off him was heavenly, utterly male, clean, sensual.

He was going to have a sore neck, too. She should wake him up. But first, she had to look her fill of him, take in the sleep-mussed hair, the lines of his face, the masculine bow of slightly parted lips.

Had she ever noticed before how long and thick his lashes were? They were sweeping the high plain of his perfect cheekbones. His stubble had thickened, dark and roguish around the line of his lips. She wanted to touch it.

And his lips.

"Hey," Molly said, softly, before she did something stupid. "Hey, *sonya*, wake up."

His eyes opened slowly. He took her in with grave surprise. His arms tightened around her waist.

"I love it when you speak Russian to me," he said, his voice a drowsy growl.

"*Sonya* means sleepyhead. Sorry, nothing sexy. You should get up and go to your own bed before you have a permanent kink in your neck."

He ignored her suggestion. "Should you and I discuss kinks? Probably not. Aw, hell, let's throw caution to the wind. Do you know anything sexy?"

She went very still. The temptation to touch the stubble on his face grew.

At the look on her face, he grinned and amended hastily, "In Russian?"

Probably better not to play with fire. "Nope, sorry."

"Ha. Could you hand me my phone? It's on the side table there."

Molly felt disappointed. One of those kind of guys, then. The first thing they did in the morning was check their phone. Well, you probably didn't get to an apartment like this by not being on top of things at your business.

He looked at his phone. He yawned. He tapped. He scrolled. Then he typed something in. Answering texts already.

CHAPTER FIFTEEN

"Everything is at our fingertips these days. I'm looking up something sexy. In Russian."

So Oscar wasn't opening texts from the office. It suddenly felt as if they were playing, but somehow an innocent game had transformed into a very dangerous one. Russian roulette.

But she could not bring herself to stop it, even though her heart was pounding, and she wanted to touch his stubble more than ever.

She nodded. Oh, sure. Why not see if it was loaded?

"You be Ursula," he said. "I'll be Dimitri."

"I don't like my name."

"Choose, then."

"Anastasia."

He raised his eyebrows as if she had said something deliberately wicked.

It was just like in the old days, when the playfulness leaped up between them as naturally as breathing. Only this had a different thrilling element to it, as if they were walking a tight-rope between the young people they had once been and the adults they now were.

In a low voice, definitely sexy, Oscar/Dimitri spoke into his phone. "You have the most beautiful eyes I've ever seen."

The phone translated, and spoke Russian to them.

"The voice is a little mechanical," Molly said. Molly was the girl who never giggled, but Anastasia didn't have that problem. "I think it scares me a bit."

"Scares you? That won't do. Here let me try to say it myself." He listened carefully to the mechanical Russian voice. He gave her a look worthy of a Cossack warrior who had galloped a white stallion across an endless steppe just to see her, and then he said the phrase. Not that she was any kind of expert in Russian, but to her his accent seemed pretty good. Not that it mattered. The tone of his voice, husky, intense, commanding, was dreamy.

"I think I'm going to swoon." Anastasia was free to say things Molly never would. And Anastasia was only partly kidding.

"Here, Ana, you try it."

She looked at the phone he handed to her. She took a deep breath. She took a risk. She looked at him. "I want to touch your stubble," she whispered into the phone, her voice hoarse.

The mechanical male voice spat it out.

"That was creepy," Oscar said, pretending horror.

She repeated what she'd heard, working the accent, blinking her lashes at him, making a little pout with her mouth. His eyes darkened. He touched his stubble. Her eyes followed his hand, yearning.

"Okay," he said, his voice a croak. "Whatever you want to touch is fine with me."

Even before the phone spat out the garbled translation, Molly, freed of her inhibitions by Anastasia, was reaching for his face.

Her fingertips scraped the rough surface of his stubble. And then her palm slid down his cheeks, cupped his chin. She closed her eyes, just letting the sensation of it sink in, the beautiful intimacy of it all. And then her fingertips trailed upward…

He stopped her hand. He held it, and held her gaze. Without saying a word, Oscar was asking her a question.

Was she sure she wanted it to go there?

Molly nodded, ever so slightly. "*Da*." She remembered the Russian word for *yes* from her childhood.

But then Anastasia gathered her cloak around

herself and faded away. Dimitri galloped off into the sunset.

Just like that, it was so real. It was Molly and it was Oscar.

"I have to tell you something," he said hoarsely. "About Cynthia."

Now?

"It wasn't about Ralphie. Not really. It was about you."

"Me?" she whispered.

"You turned my life upside down. When you left. So suddenly. Cynthia, in a way, represented everything I'd ever known. She was safe and she was predictable, and I retreated to that. But I never stopped missing the way you made me feel. Feeling like *this*—on fire with life—is what was missing."

Molly felt the fire he was talking about. She let him guide her hand to his lips. He touched her fingertips to his mouth. She explored the warmth, the softness, the texture. Ever so slowly, like a cowboy working with a wild colt, being ever so careful not to startle with the quick, unexpected move, he drew her fingertip of her index into his mouth.

His eyes never leaving her face, his tongue tangled around it. He drew gently on it, pulling it deeper into the soft cavern of his mouth.

No translation was needed for the jolt that

shot through her, white-hot. No translation was needed for the delectable weakness she felt. No translation was needed for the all-consuming hunger that licked at her as surely as his tongue had.

And no translation was needed for what happened next, either.

Oscar groaned with such helpless need, with such pent-up wanting, that Molly felt herself melt further into the thing she hated most: weakness. She felt her bone and her sinew turn to putty.

Part of her tried to warn her this was Oscar. This was her best friend. She could not risk this friendship. She had to think about tomorrow, about the future, about consequences.

But another part of her wanted only this moment with all its seductive and enchanting power.

She didn't want to be brave anymore. She wanted to surrender, to fight no more.

She acknowledged the part of her that gave up wanted something, and maybe had always wanted it. It was one of those hidden longings that became more powerful when you unleashed it.

This is what Molly wanted: something more complex than friendship, more layered, as multifaceted as a diamond.

It suddenly felt, not as if this was wrong, but as if this was the most right thing that had ever happened to her.

As if a hole inside of her made itself apparent, and with that knowledge of its existence came the knowledge that only Oscar could fill it.

Molly had a deep sense that if she did not explore this thing unfolding between them, she would spend the rest of her life—and possibly beyond, into eternity—carrying the emptiness. Feeling the void of not having known Oscar completely.

She fell toward him with the inevitability of a leaf falling to the ground in autumn.

He stood up off the couch, taking her with him, in the cradle of his arms. Carrying her easily, as if she weighed no more than a feather, he went down the hallway to his bedroom, nudged open the door with his foot, crossed the room and laid her across his huge bed.

She sank into the incredible softness of it.

Oscar stood, motionless, looking down at her with a heated gaze. As Molly watched, his hands moved to the buttons of his shirt. A smile tickled across his lips as he tormented her with slowness, flicking one button open, pausing, and then doing the next one.

Each open button revealed him to her.

She had just spent an evening with him in the swimming pool. She knew what he looked like. She had hardly been able to take her eyes off him.

But this was different.

Totally different.

Because this was a giving of himself to her and only her. This was Oscar, declaring silently, with actions rather than words, what he was about to unveil would belong to her.

Completely.

To touch. To explore. To discover. To know.

He finished with the buttons. He peeled off the shirt.

He stood there, in the half dark, holding the shirt loosely in his hand. Golden morning light was beginning to spill through the windows, gilding the broadness of his shoulder, the depth of his chest, the perfect cut of pectoral mounds, the pronounced line of his triceps, that kiss-worthy hollow at the base of his neck.

He let her look, and then Oscar let go of the shirt and it whispered to the floor. He moved to his slacks, a flick of a powerful wrist dispensing with the snap, his hand gliding down the fly. Slowly—so slowly—he slid off the pants, revealing the narrowness of his waist, the jut of his hips, the dent of his belly button, the arrow of dark hair leading her eye downward.

"You don't wear tighty-whities anymore," she squeaked.

He didn't smile. He didn't allow her to distract from the intensity of what he was revealing to her.

Instead, he bent, sliding the legs of the slacks off one at a time. He straightened and stepped out of the puddle of his discarded clothing. Her eyes trailed down the length of his legs. She shivered from the pure power of his masculine form. She looked back to his face, to see his eyes had never left her.

A smile tilted his mouth—a smile that knew what he was doing to her, that he relished it—when she licked her lips.

She could stand it no more. She held out her arms to him. With a groan of need and desire, he surrendered into them.

"Are you—"

She stopped his words with her mouth. The time for talking was done.

Oscar woke up to the sound of rain, the promise of sunshine early this morning gone, as was so often the case in this coastal city. He looked at the clock.

Had he ever slept until noon? It felt luxurious to be nestled deep into the goose down comforter, rain hammering on the windows. It felt glorious to have Molly beside him.

He got up on his elbow and looked at the woman sleeping on her side in a tangle of sheets. One arm was under the pillow, and one leg straddled the pure white squares of the comforter.

His bold and beautiful Molly.

But she had not given him that side of herself last night.

She had honored him with the other side. The hidden side. The side that sometimes he felt only he knew about, that part of her that was sweetly vulnerable, that didn't trust easily, that waited for the other shoe to drop.

The Molly that was so tender, and so sensitive. The Molly that was fragile, not strong. The Molly who might be filled with doubts this morning.

He was aware he did not want her to have a single doubt.

He tossed on a robe and tiptoed out of the room. He made coffee, and he checked on her. She was still sleeping deeply. So much for her jet-lag strategy, he thought wryly.

He didn't want her to wake up if he slipped out to get a few things, so he called the florist and the bakery. He was not sure it had ever been quite so satisfying to have enough money to do anything you wanted, to buy the contents of an entire florist shop, to order hot croissants delivered immediately.

All Oscar wanted to do was sweep that girl right off her feet.

By the time she woke, he had filled every available space in that bedroom with flowers. He had coffee and croissants on a tray for her.

Molly waking up was the cutest thing. A stir, a lapse, another stir. A blink. A stretch of one hand out from under the pillow, that slender leg finding its way back underneath the covers.

Finally, an eye opened. And then the other one.

He grinned at her.

What he saw in her face was not a single doubt.

She took him in slowly, and with wonder that made his heart go still.

"Did I die and go to heaven?" she asked huskily.

Had he made her that happy?

She set him straight. "What is that scent in here?"

Oh, so that was what was heavenly. He made a sweeping gesture to the flower-filled room.

She got up on her elbows. "What the heck?" she asked, looking around the room.

"I didn't want you to think the rain was depressing." He spoke the words into his phone. The message was redelivered to her. In Spanish.

"Depressing?" she said, her voice throaty, "It sounds like the perfect kind of day to stay in bed."

He said something really naughty into his phone. It was translated. She blushed. She laughed. She held back the covers for him. He climbed into bed with her.

"A perfect day for a trip around the world," Oscar whispered in Molly's ear, taking advantage of his close proximity to give it a little nibble. "We'll start with Spain and see how far we get."

"Okay," she agreed. "You be Bruno, I'll be Isabella."

"I don't like Bruno," he said.

"Okay, choose."

"Angelo," he said.

"Perfect. My angel." She took his phone from him. And spoke into it. He was pretty sure he blushed. Before he laughed. And then the laughter died.

When night fell, it was still raining. They had made it to Iceland, sitting in his hot tub, faces held up to the rain, pretending it was the Blue Lagoon. Bjorn and Hallveig were murmuring Icelandic endearments to each other and trying not to get the phone wet.

They fell into bed, finally, exhausted.

"It's the first day I haven't thought of Ralphie," Oscar realized, loving the feel of her head on his chest, her hair springy and wild under his fingers. "Until now. And it's weird because it's his birthday tomorrow."

"Eight months and two weeks," she said, softly, always knowing the right thing to say. "Do you feel guilty that you didn't think of him until now?"

He thought about that.

"No, his whole life was about love. He celebrated it like no one else."

There. He'd said it. Love.

He slid her a look. She didn't appear to be getting ready to run. If anything, she snuggled into him more closely.

"You're right," Molly said. "I feel like he'd be happy, as if all the pieces of the puzzle are finally in place. We couldn't give him a better birthday gift than this. Living so fully."

"That's what I think, too. That he's dancing around Uranus, beside himself with joy."

"Oh," she said happily. "We only went around the world today. Should we tackle the universe tomorrow?"

CHAPTER SIXTEEN

OSCAR FELT AS if he had been holding his breath without knowing it.

But she was the one who had mentioned tomorrow. Molly would still be here tomorrow. He allowed himself to breathe. He recognized a fear in himself, left over from their past.

He was afraid he would wake up, and without warning, she would be gone. Last time a mere kiss had driven her away. This time it had gone so much further than that.

He realized he had to address the fear.

"Why did you go?" he asked. And what he really meant was, *Will you go again?*

"I felt as if I didn't have any choice," she said, suddenly somber. "My dad had died and the farm sold. I didn't have a home anymore. I had no place to go."

He wanted to say, *I would have looked after you.* But they had both been fresh out of high school. What hope would he have had of looking after her? Still, it hurt him deeply that she had carried the double burdens—the loss of her father and suddenly being without a home—by herself.

"Photography school was suddenly an option. It hadn't been before. Even though I wanted it, I don't think Dad and I could have scraped together the money. The scholarship I got solved the problem of not having a home, and it gave me one dream to cling to, while another was gone."

"Why didn't you come to me?" he said hoarsely. "Why didn't you talk to me about it?"

"If I talked to you, I wouldn't have been strong enough to go, Truck." She hesitated for a long time.

He got up on his elbow, and saw that tears were slithering down her cheeks. He touched one. "What?" he whispered.

"You were the dream I gave up."

"The whole time I was growing up, you were solid. We moved. You stayed. We had adventures. You had routines. You were the one reliable thing. My touchstone.

"I used to think it was your mother buying the farm that made me leave, but now I'm not so sure. I'm afraid of love, Truck. Terrified of it.

"And you kissed me that night, but you, my touchstone, were already moving on. You were going to university in the fall. You had plans and ambitions, and I had few prospects. I didn't want to hold you back."

Something in him went very, very still. It wasn't that she had used the word *love* in the context of him, though he knew he would return to that later.

"My mother bought your farm?"

Her eyes went every wide. She swiped at a tear sliding down her face. "I thought you knew that," she whispered.

Oscar felt something he had rarely felt in his entire life. It was pure fury.

His mother had forced Molly's hand while she was still reeling from the death of her father. His mother had ripped Molly from his world. His mother had played on her insecurities about love.

Even those words *I didn't want to hold you back* sounded more like something his mother would say than Molly.

He remembered, suddenly, the fury deepening, that his mother had walked in on the tail end of that kiss with Molly.

And he remembered, now, that she had never once mentioned it to him.

Come to think of it, hadn't he been astonished by that? That his normally meddlesome mother had not commented on that kiss she had interrupted?

At the time, he had thought she was being sensitive, to the circumstances, to Molly's loss, to his need to comfort her.

Now, he saw it more clearly. He had said to Molly, once before, that his mother was threatened by her. The thing was, he had not realized, until this very moment, just how threatened. His mother had never once mentioned to him that she had purchased that farm. He had gone to university shortly after, so he hadn't really paid attention to what happened to the property next door to his childhood home.

Molly sensed his fury. "Don't be mad."

"I'm not mad at you."

"It's understandable from a mother's point of view," she said. "She didn't approve of me. I was the one who led you astray. Good grief, I got you arrested!"

"We swam in the public pool in the middle of the night and got caught. That's hardly a felony."

"You broke your arm because of me."

"It wasn't *because* of you."

"Uh-huh. As if you would have ever decided to jump on the back of one of Knapp's horses if I weren't around."

"Please, don't defend her," he said wearily.

"And don't *ever* do this to yourself in my presence. Make it as if you were, or are somehow, less than the Clarks. You were more than all of us put together. Do you get that? Everything you have and achieved, you did with your own guts and gumption. That's what terrified my mother. That you could be so *much.* So real. So bold. So generous. So strong. So free. And all of that came straight from inside of you. That's real power, and she knew it."

His tone softened. "And I know it. I've always known it. I see you, Molly Bentwell, I see you completely. I always have, and I always will."

She was crying really hard now. "Thank you," she whispered. "Thank you."

He took her in his arms and held her. And then, when her tears had stopped, he kissed her.

And then she kissed him back.

And then they were lost in that place where all pain was erased, and all the past, and only this moment, in all its glory, remained.

A long time later, Molly slept, and Oscar got up, and went over to the window.

Tomorrow would have been Ralphie's birthday. That's why she had come. Now, would she go? She hadn't mentioned leaving. But she hadn't mentioned staying, either.

He was not a man accustomed to being uncertain. But he was aware of feeling uncertain about this. It wasn't really about her departure date.

It was about whether or not they were feeling the same thing.

The truth tickled along his spine, and then seemed to explode, like Fourth of July fireworks inside his head.

He loved her. He didn't want to. Love involved losses and he was still reeling from Ralphie's sudden death.

Plus, Molly had already taught him about love and loss. But he had never known her reasons for leaving before. Knowing deepened what he was feeling. A quiet truth made itself known to him. It wasn't as if he had fallen in love with Molly over the last few days. It was more like he had realized he had never fallen out of love with her.

This, then, was the biggest risk of all. To love someone, even when that journey was fraught with unknown perils and unnamed dangers.

But it felt as if before he took the greatest risk of all—declaring his love to Molly—he had something else he had to look after.

With one more glance at the woman who slept in his bed—and filled his heart to overflowing—he left the room.

He went out on the deck. He didn't want Molly to overhear this call.

But, to his frustration, he only got her voice mail. "This is Amanda Clark. You know the drill. After the beep."

"I need to talk to you, *now.*" He hung up the phone.

Molly watched as Oscar listened carefully to the briefing at Zippity-Do-Da. It was like listening to the attendant go through the safety instructions before you took off on your flight. No one did it!

They had decided to do this on Ralphie's birthday. Tonight, they would go out for dinner. She had purchased the yellow dress for the occasion.

This would be good to get his mind off things. He had been carrying an undercurrent of anger since she had told him about his mother.

She looked at Oscar's familiar features, his brow furrowed in concentration. Even with that underlying current of anger, she could not look at him without feeling that rush of warmth and delight.

"Any questions?" their guide, Basil, asked.

Oscar had scientific questions. About friction. Speed. Physics. Pull. Cable strength. Regularity of cable testing. Platform testing.

She tugged at his arm. "I'm sure it's safe, Oscar."

"For your benefit, I'm going to satisfy myself."

He was the one afraid of heights, and yet he was worried about her safety. *So* endearing.

"Okay," Basil said, when he had finally managed to answer all of Oscar's questions, "if any of the following apply to you, you are not allowed to ride…"

"Please, God," Oscar murmured.

"Under five feet tall—"

"Damn."

"Heart problems—"

"Double damn."

"Pregnancy."

"I am not getting out of this, am I?" Oscar made a comical face. Normally, she would have laughed, but this time…

"Recent flu symptoms."

"How recent?"

Again, normally she would have laughed.

"Inertia. Inebriation." Basil was obviously taking his cue from Oscar and being funny now, practically reading from a medical textbook. Of course, as long as it was delaying the moment of truth—clip onto cable—Oscar was going to play along.

Typically, she might have prodded the whole

process along. But suddenly nothing felt normal. Because Molly had stopped at one word.

Pregnancy.

Good grief. She was an adult woman. A responsible woman. A woman who could absolutely not afford a pregnancy at this point in her career.

She had packed pills. She was 100 percent certain of that. She'd been supposed to start a new pack… What day? She didn't always take the "reminder" pills, just kept track of when she was supposed to start again. The travel, the jet lag—let's be honest, the drugging ecstasy of being with Oscar—might have made her careless.

Had definitely made her careless. She had not taken a pill since she arrived here, of that she was certain.

Was it really possible she had not taken a single precaution? Was it really possible that she had been so swept up in the moment that *that* had completely slipped her mind?

CHAPTER SEVENTEEN

"HEY," OSCAR CALLED to Molly. "Hey, Uranus to Earth. What's up? You're a million miles away. It's important you pay attention."

It seemed to her both of them had not been paying the least bit of attention to what was important.

He was the science guy. You'd think he could have asked that simple question about basic biology.

But then she thought of the first time, their first night together.

He had started to ask something.

Are you—

In the heat of the moment, she had assumed he was going to say *are you sure?* Or *are you ready for this?*

But, thinking about it now, both those things had been obvious, hadn't they?

No, he'd been asking her, *are you protected?*

And he'd taken her fevered response to him as a *yes* to that question.

Still, there was no need to panic. What were the chances? Probably infinitesimal. There was no sense letting it spoil this incredible time they were having together. She'd missed a few days. No biggie. She'd take one as soon as she got back to the apartment. And every day thereafter.

"Are you okay?" Oscar asked.

He had come very close to her. He was looking at her with grave concern. No one in her entire life had ever been this sensitive to her, this in tune, this caring.

"Just having a little case of nerves," she said.

He didn't tease her. He didn't say she was letting him down, and that he expected her to be the brave one. He didn't ask her where her customary boldness was.

He did what no one had ever done in her whole life. Except him.

He accepted her exactly where she was at. That was a gift she had not even been able to give herself. Instead, she was always pushing. Always proving.

He leaned in very close to her. He laid his forehead against hers. He, the guy who was terrified of heights, said quietly, for her ears only, "I got you."

She closed her eyes.

Oscar.

He'd have her back. He'd keep her safe, no matter what. It occurred to her that this man was the epitome of courage.

There was no courage, really, in doing things you had absolutely no fear of.

"I'll go first," he said. "I'll test it and make sure it's okay. And then you can follow me."

A few days ago, she would have protested that. She would have pushed her way to the front. She would have leaped first.

But now, she relaxed into this new feeling of being taken care of. Protected. Kept safe.

He turned to her just before he launched. He kissed her. Thoroughly. And then he turned and jumped.

Not with fear. There was no tension whatsoever in him. That anger that had bristled around him thankfully, and finally, appeared to be gone. After a moment, his laughter rang out, joyous, bold, off the canyon walls.

And then, at Basil's signal, Molly launched, too. And it felt as if her life—soaring through the air with the exhilarating freedom of a bird—was an exact reflection of what was going on in her heart.

Right there, right then, she knew the truth.

It was a truth that had always been there.

Like a huge Sitka spruce tree, shrouded in fog, always there, even when you couldn't see it.

And then the sun came out and burned the fog away and it stood there so majestic a person could feel foolish for having let the fog make the tree seem as if it had been an illusion.

If anything in her had been holding back, it let go now.

Her heart raced toward the man who stood on that platform in the trees, waiting to catch her.

Oscar stood out on his deck, right at the balcony, not afraid of heights at all anymore. He was annoyed that his mother still had not gotten back to him. Had she heard the anger underlying his message?

He had deeper concerns now, concerns that felt more pressing and more urgent.

He and Molly had come back from zip-lining and she had modeled her new dress for him, the one she would wear out tonight for Ralphie's birthday. He'd reserved a table at the most exclusive restaurant in Vancouver. It could take months to get a reservation, but he'd managed to pull a few strings.

It occurred to him that they had ridden bikes, eaten at food trucks, zip-lined, played in the mud and eaten pizza. All things she was comfortable with.

But they hadn't done anything fancy yet, and he was eager to explore this world with her, too. Fine restaurants. Live theater. Concerts. Charity galas. Travels. Trips.

Thoughts of the worlds they had yet to explore had then been erased from his mind, as by turns shy and confident, bold and bashful, Molly had modeled all of her other new purchases.

Until one thing led to another, and no world seemed more important than the world of two that they were in.

But then, ever so casually, just before she napped, Molly had mentioned she was going to need a bigger suitcase.

Which meant, despite it all, she was still planning on leaving.

Before Molly had arrived, it had felt to Oscar like he might never laugh again. And yet now the laughter came frequently and easily.

They had always known each other.

But now they knew each other deeply.

He could finish her sentences. She could guess his thoughts. They were unraveling the beautiful mystery of giving each other pleasure.

In that area, it felt as if they had just discovered the tip of the iceberg. It felt as if a lifetime would not be enough.

They had skirted the issue of her departure, as if hiding from it could prevent it from coming.

Now, she was talking about suitcases. He stared out at the Vancouver skyline, and it struck him like a bolt of lightning.

It was so simple. She was asking him about suitcases because he had not invited her to stay.

Invited her to stay?

That felt all wrong. Disrespectful. Without honor. As much as he wanted to have her here, he realized *this* was not what he wanted.

It was fun, yes. And exciting, definitely. Having Molly with him had turned his life into an unbelievable adventure in the seeming blink of an eye.

And yet, somehow, it wasn't sitting right with him. It had the tawdry feeling of an affair.

Oscar realized he had to show her, despite all the fun, he wasn't just playing around. He was playing for keeps.

He wanted to marry her. And the sooner the better. He wanted to spend the rest of his life with her. Thanks to his mother, they'd already lost six years.

He could almost hear his brother's voice—familiar, full of conviction—saying *go for it*.

Oscar didn't want to lose another minute.

He glanced at his watch. The stores would still be open. He could dash down now, before she woke up, and get her a ring.

He could propose to her tonight. After dinner. With her in the yellow dress.

He had to keep himself from whooping with joy and letting that whole city know what was going on with him.

Molly woke up and stretched, content. Oscar wasn't beside her, and for a moment she felt abandoned. She loved waking up with him at her side.

Still, Georgie had taken his place and having the cat in her lover's bed with her gave her an exquisite feeling of domestic contentment.

Molly realized in her whole life she might have never felt this: simple contentment. At ease with where she was. Whole in some way she had never been before. The restlessness seemed to have evaporated in her. The need to prove anything was gone. She lay there just feeling the delicious warmth of feeling accepted.

Not just by Oscar.

But by herself.

Then, she glanced at the clock, and frowned. She was really turned around. It was afternoon, nearly four o'clock. She didn't sleep in the afternoon.

It was jet lag, she told herself.

But another part of her whispered that maybe she was...

She leaped from the bed and threw on the shirt Oscar had taken off earlier. She'd take that pill, right now.

She did up the buttons on his shirt, loving how it felt on her, how it touched her thigh, and reminded her of the differences in their sizes, how perfectly their differences melded together, made them fit together.

The shirt smelled of him, and it increased that sense of belonging here and to each other.

Hadn't he even said that?

It seemed so long ago. On their first shopping excursion. There was only one time a woman should wear a man's shirt.

And this, she realized, with a sigh, was that time.

"Oscar?"

She padded out of his bedroom. The apartment was empty. She found her purse, tossed on the couch—*as if she lived here*—and picked through it for the pills. She realized, when she found them, and confirmed that she had missed starting again on the appointed day, that she didn't know a very important fact. If you were pregnant, and then resumed taking pills, could it harm the baby?

Baby.

The very thought made her go weak with longing.

She thought of that couple with their baby and Golden Retriever that she had seen on the picnic blanket that long-ago day.

To have a baby with the man you loved...

But fear rocketed through her. It would be so wrong. Backward. Oscar was a traditional kind of guy. He had even said it, and recently. He felt weddings should come before babies.

If she were pregnant, Oscar was *that* guy. The one you could trust to do the right thing.

She frowned. Did she want to be with Oscar because he was doing the right thing? She realized she was making all kinds of assumptions because of what had unfolded over the last few days.

But neither of them had said it.

The words were missing.

The *feeling* was there, Molly told herself firmly. She *knew* him.

But caring about someone and being their best friend was quite different than a declaration of love. Waking up with a sensation of belonging and completion was not a substitute for the kind of commitment that was needed to bring a new life into the world.

Molly nearly jumped out of her skin when the doorbell rang. Somehow, this apartment had felt like a small oasis, disconnected from the rest of the world. She hadn't even known it had a doorbell. The building was so secure. Somehow, she didn't think the girl guides were allowed in to go door-to-door with cookies.

She got up and tiptoed to the door and put her eye to the peephole.

Molly felt the thing she so rarely felt in her life. She swung back from the door, then told herself it couldn't be, and made herself look out the peephole again.

No, no doubt about it. It was Oscar's mother—perfectly coiffed, in a coral Chanel suit, her face suspiciously wrinkle-free—standing outside the door. Mrs. Clark rang the bell again.

"Yoo-hoo, darling," she called quietly. "I know why you called. I knew you wouldn't want to be alone today."

Molly shrank against the wall beside the door, not even daring to breathe. After her last encounter with Mrs. Clark six years ago, she didn't want Oscar's mother to see her here, and she particularly did not want to be caught running around Oscar's apartment in one of his shirts and nothing else.

She closed her eyes. A sound forced them open. *Please*, she whispered inwardly, *don't be what I think it is.*

Which was a key being inserted in the door. But under her horrified gaze, Molly watched as the lock turned.

CHAPTER EIGHTEEN

THE DOOR SQUEAKED OPEN, and Mrs. Clark swept into the room in a cloud of perfume. Georgie, who had been sleeping on the couch, startled awake, glared at the intruder and then, with an indignant yowl—Molly was not sure if it was recognition—leaped from the couch and marched from the room, tail in the air.

Mrs. Clark watched the cat with naked dislike and then saw Molly, still tucked against the wall beside the door. Her mouth formed a perfect, surprised O. But her surprise didn't last very long. Her eyes narrowed.

"Molly Bentwell," she said, managing to load Molly's name with enough disapproval that Molly cringed inwardly, though she let nothing—she hoped—show outwardly.

"Mrs. Clark," she said evenly.

"I thought you were half a world away," Mrs. Clark said, disparagingly. "Taking pictures of monkeys, or something."

A whole career dismissed in one hateful sentence.

"I do wildlife photography," Molly said, keeping her tone level, despite the fact she was seeing red. "It's a little more complex than taking pictures of monkeys."

Mrs. Clark waved a hand, as if a fly had landed on her nose. "Really, it's exactly the kind of work I always expected you would find."

How was she making a perfectly respectable profession seem as if it were somehow lacking respectability?

Of course, respectability in Mrs. Clarks's world would be very narrowly defined.

"Can I ask what you are doing trotting around my son's apartment in an outfit like that?"

There was her narrow definition of respectable, right there. Molly could feel her cheeks burning. How dare Mrs. Clark cast the situation with Oscar in that light? As if it were cheap, and impulsive and base?

And yet, by appearances alone, would it not seem as if Mrs. Clark were correct.?

"Always the train wreck, Molly," Mrs. Clark said, with a sad shake of her head. "Hardly a week went by without you leading my poor Oscar on some kind of misguided escapade. Police, arrests, hospital visits, mischief reports from school. We just aren't the kind of people who enjoy that kind of activity and attention."

We.

With Molly Bentwell on one side of the great divide, and the Clarks on the other. All the Clarks. Did it hurt so much because there was truth in it?

"I'd ask again you what you're doing here," Mrs. Clark said, her gaze sweeping Molly, "but now it's perfectly obvious. You've started up right where you left off, it would appear. Why would you horn in to our family at a time like this, though? Especially today. It's unbelievably cheap and insensitive to insert yourself in our pain over Ralph. Of course, I wouldn't expect *you* to know some events are sacred within families."

"What does that mean?" Molly asked, even though she knew she was going to be sorry she had.

Mrs. Clark sighed. "I'm not without sympathy for you, Molly, I'm really not. I mean your father..." Her voice drifted off. "You really were like a child raised by a wolf. It's no wonder you have so few skills. It's no wonder you look at what we have and would go to any length to get it."

"My father did the best he knew how," she said tersely.

"Of course he did, dear," Mrs. Clark said, her soothing tone belying her total insincerity.

"I remember my childhood with extreme affection."

"What child wouldn't? The lack of rules, no structure, bad behavior *encouraged*. Your father thought it was hilarious when the two of you were arrested."

"For breaking into a swimming pool, after hours," Molly reminded her.

"One thing does lead to another."

"But it didn't."

"Oh, I don't know. Then he broke his arm. Riding horses he did not have permission to ride."

Who saw adolescent hijinks through this lens?

"I did not horn in on your grief for Ralphie. Oscar invited me here."

In fact, she could see that one line of his email. *Come.* She wanted to cling to it, as if it were a lifeline.

"Don't you know when someone is merely being polite?"

Suddenly, Molly saw there was no sense trying to convince Mrs. Clark of her worthiness. That boat had sailed a long time ago. It was not helped by the fact she was now standing barefoot in front of her lover's mother in a state of undress.

"I'll just go get dressed," she said woodenly.

When she reappeared a few minutes later, she was caught up short as she entered the living room. Mrs. Clark was sitting on the sofa.

And she had Molly's phone in her hand.

Her mouth was twisted in a sneer of complete contempt. "Your search engine was open," she said. "It seems you were researching pregnancy."

"It's extraordinarily rude to snoop through other people's phones," Molly said.

Mrs. Clark appeared unchastised. "It's just as I feared all those years ago. You were intent on trapping him then, and you are intent on trapping him now."

There was, of course, the desire to explain, the need to be respected, and accepted. She loved Oscar. Naturally, she wanted the approval of his mother.

But she could see in those hardened features that was the one thing she would never get from Mrs. Clark.

"What will it cost me this time?" his mother said with a sigh.

To get rid of her.

It would be insulting, except that Molly had allowed herself to be bought all those years ago. And now, she *had* risked a pregnancy, the very thing she felt she had been falsely accused of.

Maybe there was the awful possibility Mrs. Clark saw her more clearly than she saw herself.

Her *need* for everything Oscar offered. Stability. Security. Protection. Acceptance. Love.

But Mrs. Clark already saw that Molly would never fit in his world. Never. That would be the price for him if he accepted her love.

And now, because she might be pregnant, she would never know. She had been reckless, careless, just like her father… Everything that this woman sitting before her despised.

She would never know if Oscar would have turned his back on his world for love of her.

Or if he would have done it only because there might be a baby.

Either way, she could not ask that kind of sacrifice of him. She loved him. And she didn't want him to have to give up anything, let alone the respect and acceptance of his whole world, because of her.

Without a word, Molly went and held out her hand. Mrs. Clark placed the phone in it.

"It won't cost you anything to get rid of me," Molly said quietly. "I don't want anything to do with you or from you. I find it funny that you think I would want anything you have. I always felt sorry for Oscar and Ralph, being part of your soulless world that always had to look so good. And that always felt so bad."

"You felt sorry for my children?" Mrs. Clark said, something satisfyingly shrill in her voice. "Why, you little…upstart."

Allowing herself the satisfaction of that tiny victory, Molly went back to her room and packed her bag. She put only the things in it she had come with. Assuming his mother would be in the guest room, she carefully made the bed, and took everything else. She went into his room and stuffed it way in the back of his closet.

This time together with Oscar was going to be hard enough to get over without reminding herself of him every time she put on her underwear.

It would only serve to remind her, too, of who she had become when she was with him.

Georgie was in the middle of his bed. Molly went and sank down just briefly, held her cat to her, and felt the deep purr calm her and give her the strength she needed. She set the cat down.

She would not cry. She would be the girl her father had always wanted her to be: proud, fierce, independent.

Bentwells were not sissies.

Not even if their hearts were breaking in two.

Putting her bag over her shoulder, she took a deep breath, and put her chin up. She sailed out through the living room and out the door without a single glance back at Mrs. Clark.

* * *

Oscar burst back into his apartment. It had taken longer than he expected to find the ring. He wanted it to be perfect.

And for Molly, that would mean nothing garish. Nothing too large. Nothing ostentatious. It had taken him three jewelry stores until he had found exactly the right one, a beautiful simple band, with a single small solitaire, multifaceted and brilliant—just like Molly—winking at its center.

Tonight, after dinner, he would ask her. He went over it in his mind. In the restaurant? Maybe he could have the ring hidden in a dessert dish, or a rose. Or would she'd like it better if, as they were walking home, hand in hand, he just fell down on one knee? And after she said yes, they'd come back here to the apartment, and he'd show her how to dance. Maybe on the deck, beside the pool, under the stars.

It could give new meaning to dancing with the stars. He couldn't wait to make her laugh by saying that to her.

"Molly!" He stopped in the doorway. Some strange fragrance tickled his nostrils. For a moment, he thought, *I know that scent.* Definitely not Molly…but his desire to see her made him dismiss anything that was not her.

"Molly!"

His voice rang back at him. Surely she wasn't still sleeping? He went into his bedroom. The bed was rumpled, and the cat was there, but Molly wasn't. He raced to her room. Empty. The bed was neatly made. She clearly hadn't slept in it for a while. He cocked his head, listening for the shower. Nothing.

He raced through the apartment and out to the pool.

But Molly wasn't anywhere. He went back to the spare bedroom. It struck him, suddenly, that it felt empty. He didn't see her bag. He went and opened a bureau drawer. Empty.

Where was Molly? It felt as if that was all that mattered to him. He took out his cell phone and texted her.

Maybe he hadn't been abandoned. There was probably an explanation. She had gone to get something to surprise him tonight, just as he had her.

And she took her travel bag with her to do it? a cynical voice inside of him said.

It hit him then, and it hit him hard.

It was his brother's birthday. Molly was gone. He didn't think he could get through the next hours, days and weeks carrying the burden of the loss.

CHAPTER NINETEEN

MOLLY SAT IN the airport lounge, waiting for a flight. The pings started coming on her phone, fast and furious.

All of the messages were from Oscar.

Where are you? What happened? What's going on?

Obviously, there was no point in honesty here. She couldn't exactly say *your mother thinks I'm a tramp, and that I'm trying to entrap you. And I might be pregnant, so maybe she's right.*

She could discern the frantic worry in each of his messages, so she texted back.

So sorry to leave on such short notice. I've had some business things come up that I have to look after. It was urgent.

Are you kidding me? No goodbye? Just out the door?

You know me…a little lacking in social graces. Don't get me wrong, I had a glorious time.

It's his birthday.

For a moment, weakness nearly doubled her over. It *was* Ralphie's birthday. They *had* to be together. That had been the plan, all along.

Her father had been right. His entire life he had scorned plans.

And this was why. They went awry. Tentatively, she responded.

Your mother suggested I was intruding on a private family moment.

He didn't answer and her phone began to ring instantly. She suddenly felt weary, emotionally wrung out.

Just like last time, his mother had given her an excuse to do what she wanted to do, anyway. Run from the terrible complexities, the potential for pain, of loving someone the way she loved Oscar.

Her phone began ringing again and then went to voice mail.

Oops, there's my plane. Till next time.

She shut off her phone. She laid her head on the back of the chair. And she wept. And when she was done, she wiped her eyes, blew her nose and vowed that was it.

It was not as if she had not done this before. Left him when it felt as if it would tear her in two to do it.

And if her father had given her a gift, it was this one: she was tough, and she was resilient. She could outrun anything if she had to.

She filled the days that followed by moving. Moving was always an excellent antidote for pain. Changing countries made it even more complex. She threw a dart at a map.

Oslo, Norway.

Why not? What did it matter? Her father would have approved.

The pregnancy test came back negative, but warned her it could give a false negative if she took it too early.

She went on assignment in Africa. No nausea, no headaches, no exhaustion, despite moving and jet lag.

She took the test again, still negative.

Her new neighbors in Oslo had a baby. She took photos of it. Their friends wanted a session. And then their friends wanted a session. And then *their* friends wondered if she would think about doing a wedding...

Her period came.

Molly didn't feel relieved. Not at all. Her sense of loss and grief intensified.

She started canceling assignments to do baby pictures. She thought the babies might be a trigger, but in fact, she loved immersing herself in baby smiles, and baby fat, and baby toys, and baby smells.

Slowly, it dawned on her that while leaving Oscar had broken her in two, something about those days with him had made her better.

When she looked at her work, Molly saw a new dimension to it. Something in her was more open than it ever had been, and it showed in her photos.

They were warmer, kinder, softer.

Somehow, she was capturing a light in people that she had never captured before. She was digging deeper.

Even though she had walked away from love, the irony was that she felt as if she was on intimate terms with love for the first time.

It was when she was not working that the memories would hit.

Oscar in his chef's apron. Oscar with pomegranate on his face. Oscar covered in mud.

Oscar riding a bike, leaping off a zip line, lying in the grass beside her.

But that was the place she could not go.

Oscar lying beside her.

That was what she missed the most. Her world had gone from wholly complete to wholly empty, from total bliss to total despair.

In the blink of an eye.

She learned to distract herself at the first twinge of a memory. She could watch a movie, as long as it wasn't a romantic one. Hockey games were great. So was playing word games on her phone, or watching talent shows. She could chat online about photography.

She could make it okay. She could make life bearable.

As long as she did not think of his eyes.

His smile.

His deep voice whispering in her ear.

His lips on her hair.

And on her lips.

And on her...

Damn. She was crying again. The strong one, the resilient one, a hot mess of emotion. It seemed totally unfair to be this emotional, without the pregnancy.

A knock came on the door. Everything in Molly froze. Maybe he had come. But why would he? She had run out on him, not once, but twice. In his heart, he probably knew, just as his mother did, that he was better off without her.

So, who then?

She got up and looked out her peephole. It felt like déjà vu. Mrs. Clark was standing outside her door. For a moment, Molly considered not answering it. What had Oscar's mother ever brought her other than pain?

But there was something about her that was not the same. Her hair was disheveled. Her makeup was smudged.

What if something had happened to Oscar?

Molly flung open the door.

"Oh, Molly, thank goodness. It's been so hard to find you." His mother—his self-contained, controlled mother—burst into tears.

"What's wrong? Is Oscar okay?"

"N-n-n-o-o-o," she wailed. "I've lost both my sons."

"He's—?"

"No, no, he's not dead. But he might as well be."

Molly's heart went into her throat. She fought down the pure panic she was feeling, ushered her in and set her on her sofa. Her heart was beating out of her chest.

"Mrs. Clark, please tell me why you have

come around the world to find me. And please tell me Oscar is okay."

"I've come around the world to find you because I couldn't very well ask Oscar for your phone number. And, anyway, I needed to speak to you in person. I need you to understand and I wasn't sure I could convey that on the phone."

"Understand?" Molly whispered, still trying to fight down panic.

"He's not okay. He won't even speak to me now. He's not going into the office. I sent Cynthia to check on him. He wouldn't let her in, but she said he looked horrible! His place was a catastrophe. She could see it behind him, even though he was blocking the door.

"It's all my fault. He won't forgive me. I pretended I hadn't been there when you left. I pretended I had just showed up.

"But he said he could smell my perfume. He *knew*. When I told him I felt you were unsuitable, Molly, he lost his mind. And then he told me he knew about the other time, too. About me buying your farm.

"I've never seen him like that. He was nasty. He said my world had never brought him one moment's happiness. He said all the rules, looking a certain way, acting a certain way, getting a degree, achieving success, having anything money can buy, finding a woman who fits in that world—he said none of that had brought him one moment of happiness. He said it was all a complete illusion."

Mrs. Clark looked imploringly at Molly. "Do you think that's true? Not one moment's happiness?"

"Of course not," Molly said soothingly.

"He even accused me of not loving Ralphie. He said I had no idea what love was. That it wasn't about manipulating people to get them to meet your needs."

Mrs. Clark took a huge shuddering breath. "And he's right," she said. "Even when you were children, I saw the way he looked at you. The way you looked at him. You put out the sun in each other's worlds every morning and drew down the moon at night. I wasn't jealous. I wasn't. But…"

Her voice drifted away, and then came back stronger. "I wasn't jealous, but maybe scared. He was right about love. His father and I didn't have one of those warm, cozy relationships. I had my boys and they gave me a sense of purpose. They made my world feel justified and important. Oscar, in particular, was so bright, and had so much potential. It felt like a reflection on me.

"But I could feel him moving toward a different world. The one you held out. And I tried to stop it.

"Oh, Molly, I tried to stop my son's happiness to meet my own needs. He was right about me, wasn't he? Not that that matters. I don't matter. I've made my mistakes and I'll live with the consequences.

"But I don't want him to live with the consequences. To be unhappy forever because of what I've done. He won't come to you, Molly. He won't. Because he wants you to choose. He *needs* you to choose."

"Of course, I choose him," Molly said.

"He doesn't need you to choose him. He needs you to choose yourself."

And just like that, Molly saw the truth in what Mrs. Clark was saying. She needed to make the choice to overcome all of her insecurities. All of her fear. All of her self-doubts.

To rescue Oscar, she needed to be more than she had ever been before. What had passed as bravery before would not do for this assignment.

And she could not have a single reservation left about love. To save Oscar—and herself— she had to throw herself at the mercy of the most powerful force in the entire universe.

When Oscar woke up his mouth tasted gritty and his hair felt caked to his head. Someone was knocking at the door. He closed his eyes and willed himself back to sleep.

Except he heard the door open, the tap of footsteps coming down the hall.

He braced himself. Only two people had keys to his apartment. His mother and Cynthia. He did not want to see either of them.

But it wasn't either of them.

It was Molly, in travel clothes, her hair springing up on one side of her head and crushed on the other. She didn't have on a speck of makeup.

And he had never seen a woman look so beautiful.

Not that he could let her know. Ever.

He loved control and he had found the perfect way to control the whole world. And that was not to engage with it.

Molly was not going to threaten the thing that was most precious to him, ever again.

"What do you want?" he growled.

"I hope that smell isn't you," she said. "Poor Georgie. When's the last time you changed the litter?"

Maybe his world wasn't quite as controlled as he thought.

She marched over and opened his drapes. The light flooded in, hurting his eyes. She turned and looked at him. What he saw in her eyes—the softness, the understanding, the connection to him—could make a weaker man give up on control forever.

But he had been weak. He had given up on control. He had fallen for Molly when he knew better. It had not had the result he wanted. And he was still enough of a scientist not to do the same thing over and over again expecting different results.

"Why are you here?" he asked.

That traitor cat had found his way out from under a mess of blankets and meowed a greeting at her. She went and picked him up, and he snuggled against her, purring rapturously as if there were no abandonment to be forgiven.

"I came," she said softly, "because I couldn't stay away."

"Huh. You wouldn't have had to stay away if you hadn't left in the first place."

"Truck, I thought I was pregnant."

He sat straight up in bed. He was out of his fog in an instant, staring at her. "Are you?" he whispered.

"No. It's probably a good thing. Can you imagine me raising children?"

He could, actually.

"I can imagine you raising children," he told her. "I'm sorry you aren't pregnant."

CHAPTER TWENTY

MOLLY GAZED AT OSCAR—at the unshaven face, the rumpled hair, the sharpness of his cheek-bones.

I'm sorry you aren't pregnant.

"Isn't that lucky for all of us?" Molly said. "Me *not* having a baby?"

She kept out of her voice how she had wept when she had seen the *negative* flash across the little screen.

It wasn't until that moment that she'd realized how totally selfish she could be—if she couldn't have Oscar, she had wanted his baby.

Even knowing she would be the world's most unlikely mother.

"Maybe we could talk about babies in a minute," he suggested, and Molly heard some tenderness in his tone that made her want to melt into him when she most needed to be strong. "I want to sort out the past, before we tackle the future."

The future. Her strength felt as if it abandoned her a little bit more.

"My mother told me it was her behind you leaving."

"I thought she was right, Oscar," Molly said quietly, marshalling what was left of her strength, after a long soul-searching trip. "That I couldn't fit into your world. That I'm just kind of a wild girl from the wrong side of the tracks—"

"Then why are you here?"

"Because I realized it wasn't really about her and whether she was right or wrong. It was about me. All my life, I've been rewarded for being brave, for taking chances. And yet, the greatest risk of all filled me with terror. I looked for any excuse to run from it. So, that's what I did. I used your mother as an excuse to run from what my heart was telling me."

"What was your heart telling you?" he asked. His voice was so gentle, so safe. She was coming home, finally, to her Truck. She was one truth away.

"It was telling me the only truth worth knowing. That I love you. Past. Present. Future. The possibility of a baby confused everything. Would you feel honor-bound to do the decent thing? It felt like a baby would remove *choice* from the equation."

"Choice," he said hoarsely. "Baby or no baby, I would never choose a world without you. Why would I want that? That hurts me. That you would know me so well—maybe better than anyone else on earth—and yet you would think that keeping the stuff in my world, all the trappings of success, would mean more than you… I would rather live under a bridge, in a cardboard box, with you, than live in a world without you. That's how alive you make me feel. How full to the top."

"There's so much I don't know," she warned him. "I don't know the rules everyone else plays by. You do. You had a place where the rules were clearly defined. A place where dinner was always ready at the same time. You had a place where if you got arrested, people were appalled rather than applauding. What can I give children? I can't even keep a plant alive. I don't know how to bake cookies. I tend to see a kitchen counter as a great place to store cameras and parts. I think a *great* supper is potato chips with a side of onion dip. I—"

Oscar stepped in close to her. The look in his eyes mesmerized her. He laid a finger across her lips.

"Stop it," he ordered her softly. "Did you come here thinking I would listen to your arguments and be convinced you're somehow wrong for me?"

"I just want you to know *exactly* what you are getting into."

"Oh, I already know exactly what I'm getting into. Do you think I don't know what you'd be like with a family? With children? I've watched you for years.

"I watched you with your dad. I saw your fierce loyalty to him. You loved him unconditionally, flaws and all. What a gift that would be to give children.

"And I watched you with Ralphie. Of all the people who knew him, you were the one always coaxing him to be himself, rewarding him for being himself, loving him for being himself.

"And the whole swim team—gathering them around you, making the hardest things fun, making them into a family, for each other, for you, for us.

"I've watched you with Georgie, ever since he was a little scared kitten, teaching him it was okay to trust, and okay to love.

"And most of all, Molly, I've watched you with me, taking my rigid thinking and bending it on its ear. Challenging me—to take risks, to press boundaries, to challenge truth, to be more than I ever was before."

He turned from her and took something off

his bedside table. "I've been sleeping with this beside me. Tormenting me, but also giving me hope."

He came back to her.

"I can't live without you," he said. He went down on one knee. "This isn't how I planned it, Molly, but I've always known, with you, things don't go as planned. Sometimes, they are so much better than anything I could have dreamed."

Her hands flew to her mouth and covered it as Oscar—her Truck—held out a velvet ring box.

He snapped open the lid.

"I bought this on Ralphie's birthday," he said softly. "I was going to propose that night, at dinner. I didn't want to waste another six years without you."

"Do you really feel as if those years were wasted?" she asked him through tears.

"Yes!"

"I feel so differently. I feel as if it showed me what I most needed to see—how empty a life without you would be. I think those six years might be what are making me brave enough to say yes, Truck."

"I haven't asked you yet!"

"Yes!" she said, again.

"Would you wait? I have the most romantic—"

"I'm not waiting," she said, "I don't regret the six years, but I'm not waiting one more minute."

And then she launched herself at him, and knocked him off his knee and they were on the floor with her on top of him, covering his face with kisses.

And Oscar was aware, for all of his planning, he could not have imagined a more romantic ending to his proposal than this one.

EPILOGUE

OSCAR COULD FEEL the faint pleasurable burn in his legs as he climbed the high hill. The baby, thankfully, had finally fallen asleep inside the kangaroo pouch Oscar had strapped to his chest.

Ralph—unlike his big sister, three-year-old Harriet—was a difficult baby.

"Can't we put him back?" Harriet had asked this morning, when the crankiness had started.

"Um, that would be a little painful for your mother," Oscar had said, and slid Molly a look. His wife. His partner. She seemed to grow more beautiful each day, even now with this fractious new edition intent on keeping the whole family from sleep.

"I'll take him for a walk," Oscar had volunteered. Being stuffed into the snuggly baby carrier seemed to be the only thing that soothed the crabby baby. Molly shot him a grateful look, and Harriet, having had quite enough of the baby brother, did not even volunteer to join him.

Now, the baby slept, finally, and Oscar found a rock and perched on it, taking in the spectacular view with wonder. He could hear Walter—a donkey Molly had rescued—braying incessantly, every bit as demanding as the new baby when it came to his feeding schedule.

Below him, looking like toys in a giant's game, was his mother's property: the sweeping grounds, the white colonial style mansion, the sparkling waters of the pool, the clipped hedges, the rose garden, the trimmed lush pastures. Even from this height, it was evident everything was manicured, ordered into place.

And next to that was Molly's farm.

Their farm now, since Oscar had bought it back from his mother. This is where they came when they needed a break from everything. They could have gone and skied the Alps, or lounged on some of the best beaches in the world. They could have gone to Paris and explored little cafés and strolled the banks of the Seine. They could have gone on safari in Africa.

But no, more and more, they came here. And each time, it seemed they stayed a little longer and were a little more reluctant to head back to Vancouver.

From his vantage point, so high above it, Oscar could see Molly's childhood home had come a long way from what it had been. The house was looking good, painted white, the wraparound porch, with its deeply cushioned furniture, looking cool and inviting. Three small cozy cabins had been built, and dotted the wooded area behind the house. Molly was putting the pieces in place to host photography retreats, someday.

Still, for all the improvements, he could see the property needed a lot of work. The pasture was weed-filled. The fence was leaning haphazardly. The barn looked as if a good wind would take it down. A dead tree needed to be looked after.

Possibly a lifetime's worth of work. For some reason, that increased Oscar's sense of contentment.

Inch by inch, day by day, she was uncovering the true beauty of the house that had gone a bit to ruin over six years of being uninhabited. When Oscar had seen that the roof had leaked and rodents had gotten inside, he had thought maybe they should just tear it down and start again.

But, no, she saved things. Just like she had saved him.

She was showing what was underneath the

water-damaged ceilings, what was underneath the peeling wallpaper and what was underneath the vinyl floors that had been curling at the corners. She had discovered shiplap and original hardwoods and custom tile work. The walls had hidden fireplaces and someone, sometime, had decided it was a good idea to cover up a stained glass window with a wall.

It seemed to Oscar that Molly worked the same magic on him as she was working on that house. Inch by inch, day by day, she was uncovering him, showing him what was underneath, revealing who he really was, *loving* what was underneath the layers he had built up over the years.

From the first day they had come back here, Molly had thrown open the doors to anyone who wanted to come. And so, on any given day, members of the old swim team might drop by—or the new one that swam now, in the swim pavilion named after his brother.

James lived in one of the little cottages behind the house, and acted as their caretaker when they weren't here. The neighbors came by, and old friends from school. The grill was fired up. The campfire was lit in the pit behind the house. Sometimes, guitars came out and the music and laughter and conversation went deep into the night.

They were forming a community.

That's what family really was.

As he watched, from his perch high up on the hill, Oscar saw Molly and Harriet come out of the house. Harriet was carrying a basket of carrots for Walter in one hand and skipping ahead of her mother. Today, she was wearing a pink princess dress and wielding a plastic pirate's sword in her other hand. Her hair was dark like his but her springy curls were just like her mother's and made attaching the toy tiara nearly impossible. It sat on her head crookedly.

Walter's braying increased in volume, hysteria and intensity when he spotted the little girl skipping toward him.

And then out of the corner of Oscar's eye, he saw his mother coming down the well-worn path between the two properties.

There was a spring in her step, as if she were moving eagerly toward all that chaos. Not that she would ever admit it. No, she would get there and complain about the noise the donkey made, and remove the crooked tiara, and run a disapproving hand through Harriet's tangled curls. She would get a pinched expression on her face when she noticed the flowerbeds were now almost completely taken over with weeds.

After his mother's treachery toward Molly,

Oscar would have been just as happy to keep her at a distance.

But Molly wasn't having it.

She paved the way to forgiveness even as she came into herself, or maybe it was because she came into herself so completely that Molly was able to extend such grace to others.

After he had told his mother he and Molly were going to get married, Mrs. Clark had tried to take over the wedding.

"It can't be trusted to a girl who doesn't even know how to use the right fork," she'd said, and thrown herself into choosing guests and a posh venue that specialized in the weddings "of anybody who was anybody."

Gently and firmly, Molly, the girl who didn't even know how to use the right fork, had vetoed that. They had been married in that falling down barn right over there.

He still could not think of the merriment, the utter joy of that day, without smiling. Molly, the one who had *hated* dancing, had danced until dawn.

"Your poor mom," she had told him. "Something made her life that. So rigid, so bound by rules, so worried about what everything looks like. She's afraid of being real. But she's also very, very brave."

Slowly, he had watched Molly's love transform his mother.

Just as it transformed everything around her. She had started doing photo shoots here. With chickens and the donkey, with falling down fences, and overgrown pastures as the backdrop. Georgie loved to stalk out of the house and photobomb the sessions.

Celebrities had discovered her and flocked to her with their children, and always, she gave them what they wanted.

Her gift was capturing the perfect against the backdrop of imperfection. She captured the light inside of people.

And it didn't really matter if it was a celebrity shoot, or the new Special Games swim team, or a single mom with a new baby.

This was Molly's gift. She no longer had to face a charging elephant to get the perfect shot, or edge too close to the cliff, or hang from her knees from the tallest tree branch.

She no longer had to do those death-defying things to *feel*. She had faced a greater fear— that love would let her down—and she had won, and now she brought that out in others.

She found the love that lit people up from within. It didn't matter how deeply they had buried it, or how hard they tried to hide it.

She found it.

And for being the recipient of that, of Molly's spectacular gift, Oscar would be forever grateful.

Ralph, suddenly aware the walk had stopped, woke up with a roar. Oscar got to his feet, swaying back and forth with the baby.

It was time to go join whatever was going on down there today. Were they painting a picket fence, or weeding a garden, or taking a picnic into the woods?

The baby, Ralphie's namesake, often made Oscar feel as if his brother were close to him. Right now, it felt as though the wind had whispered to him in his brother's voice.

Go for it.

He said the words out loud.

It felt so good, he shouted them from the top of that hill, listened to them roll down the landscape around him.

Startled, the baby quieted, arched his back, and looked at his father as if he recognized something in him for the first time.

He gurgled. It sounded, well, approving.

Go for it.

It didn't mean win a medal, or make a million dollars.

It meant embrace whatever the day put in front of you.

Completely.

It meant, live well. Love well.

And as he headed back down the hill toward his farm, toward his family, that was exactly what Oscar intended to do.

* * * * *

If you enjoyed this story, check out these other great reads from
Cara Colter

Matchmaker and the Manhattan Millionaire
One Night with Her Brooding Bodyguard
Cinderella's New York Fling
Cinderella's Fairytale Millionaire

All available now!